FIC
McK      McKinley, James.
             The fickleman
         suite and other

7/94

T

# The Fickleman Suite

AND OTHER STORIES

# The Fickleman Suite

## AND OTHER STORIES

## James McKinley

THE UNIVERSITY OF ARKANSAS PRESS
FAYETTEVILLE 1993

97  96  95  94  93      5  4  3  2  1

*This book was designed by Ellen Beeler using the typefaces Garamond and Bodoni.*

The paper used in this publication meets the minimum requirements of the American National Standard for Permanence of Paper for Printed Library Materials Z39.48-1984. ⊚

*Library of Congress Cataloging-in-Publication Data*

McKinley James.
    The fickleman suite and other stories / James McKinley.
        p.  cm.
    Contents: House call — The novice writer explores cartography — Moriarty's true colors — Moriarty's spells — Liebestod — A post-modern instance — The fickleman suite — Memorial Day — Moon in cancer.
    ISBN 1-55728-238-2 (alk. paper). — ISBN 1-55728-239-0 (pbk.: alk. paper)
    I. Title.
    PS3563.C3815F5   1993
    813'.54—dc20                            92-4515
                                        CIP

"A Fickleman Jogs" and "Praying for a Fickleman" are reprinted by permission of Breitenbush Books, Inc., P.O. Box 02137, Portland, Oregon 97202.
"Liebestod" was first printed in *Story Quarterly,* Chicago, Illinois.
"The Novice Writer Explores Cartography" is reprinted by permission of *New Letters,* Curators of the University of Missouri, Kansas City, Missouri.

# Contents

# House Call

*Rosebud Reservation, South Dakota: November 1917*

Between the babies crying and the groans of the smelly old squaws, Edna West Henderson was just about to go berserk. Bad enough that she was stuck in this ancient, cold house, with snow piled all around and a leaky wood stove to stoke and coal-oil lamps to fill, linens to wash and instruments to boil and their meals to fix. Worse, she'd missed two periods, and she was regular as a school clock, so there was little doubt she was pregnant, even if she didn't feel too nauseated or for that matter different at all. Except bored and tired. Days like this she wished she was back in the parsonage with her foster parents, even if they were strict. But then, naturally, she wouldn't be married to Jerry, and that did make up for some things. She guessed she'd tell him tonight. He never noticed physical things about her, hardly, which was odd since as a doctor he noticed just about everything about these darned Indians.

Edna checked her boiling pot. Jerry's instruments lay in the bubbling water. The heat and vapor had frosted the windows so that she couldn't see out. Didn't matter. Nothing but snow and the few other houses of this wonderful town of White River. Edna picked up her copy of *McClure's* and dreamed again. One day, she vowed, she'd live in a grand house as these ladies did, and serve tea, and wear gowns and give fancy parties at home and at the country club, and have shiny, expensive automobiles instead of the old flivver that the Indian agent had lent Jerry, that and his old team of horses good only for glue and to get up the trails into where the Lakota Sioux lived in those horrid clapboard government houses or their smoky tipis with what they traveled with. Might as well be gypsies. Edna just knew she was born for better than what she had now, but she reminded herself, looking at the lovely long dresses sketched in the magazine, that she was only nineteen and there was a war on. Better, she supposed, to be here doctoring the Indians than have Jerry on the Western Front. But, maybe not. For a moment she pictured herself getting the telegram and weeping over her heroic dead husband, killed while doing valiant duty in a field hospital, and she could see herself beautiful in black at the funeral with all the soldiers shooting into the air, and the flag, and the white granite cross with Jerry's name on it. And didn't war widows get some money, too? But Jerry's eyesight wasn't good enough for the medical corps, whatever eyes had to do with it. So they were here. Besides, if she were pregnant, that would ruin the whole pretty picture.

"Edna? Edna, are they ready? I need them."

Jerry's voice wrenched Edna back to White River. She dropped *McClure's* on the kitchen table, carefully picked up the pot, and poured the water into the sink. Carrying the pot with a towel she walked to the front parlor where Jerry had established his treatment room. She stepped on tiptoes past the Indians hunched in the hall against the wall. The smell of grease and sweat and whiskey wrinkled her nose. She shouldered back the half-open parlor door.

"Here, darling," Edna said.

Jerome Henderson looked up from his patient, to be struck again by his young wife's beauty. She positively glowed, from her swept-up auburn hair to her tiny feet, and all between pleased him, not least the curves of bosom and hips. In this forsaken place, amongst these poor, ailing and alien natives, she shone like a beacon guiding him to happiness. Well, Jerome corrected himself, certainly happiness as much as could be had here. But she put up with all this so well, and it helped both of them knowing it was just a first job, all he could get right out of Creighton Medical School. A house, a practice, an automobile. Not too bad, really. And certainly all he could want in the way of medical experience. These people had every disease known to him, many courtesy of the whites who'd invaded these lands. Progress. Jerome admitted there was medical progress, and industrial and maybe artistic, but look at the war. Poison gas. Tons of artillery shells that tore, maimed, killed. What was it? Four million dead so far on both sides? Progress.

"Wonderful, dear. Put them there, will you?" He watched Edna's graceful move to the instrument case. They'd taught her well at Reverend Gray's. She moved like a lady, knew how to cook and sew and what silverware to use. Rather remarkable, actually.

"How many are out there?" Jerome asked.

"The hall's full, and the front bedroom, too."

"Looks like a thundering day again. But I'll hurry. I promise."

Edna's smile flashed across to him, and then she was out

the door headed toward her chores. Poor girl, but nineteen, tending to the household and feeding the team when he didn't have time, going with him when he needed her out into the reservation. Jerome hoped the winter wouldn't be too severe, though it was starting out like a bitch kitty. It was their first, and the agent warned them about getting stuck on the trails. You'll freeze quicker than water, he'd said. Find you in the spring, hard as rock candy. Well, she was sweet enough anyway.

Jerome turned his attention to the patient, a Lakota woman of some middling age. He couldn't tell, and they never said. She had a boil the size of a walnut on the back of her neck, glowing raw red against her coppery skin. Henderson painted the area with tincture of iodine.

"This will hurt. I have to cut. You understand?" He moved the side of his hand like a knife.

The woman nodded and bowed her head. Strange, he thought, these people. In the six months he'd been here he'd seen them bear hideous pain with scarcely a murmur. Women in childbirth. Men with knife wounds in their guts. Even dying from the influenza raging everywhere, as so many were despite what he could do, they stayed silent until the death rattle shook them. Then the women started to keen and there was plenty of noise, but before that it was like they had a pact with the Great Spirit to endure life's sufferings with dignity. Whites didn't, at least the ones he'd treated during his internship in Omaha.

Jerome took the newly boiled scalpel and the draining cup. With a quick, deft stroke he sliced into the infection. The pus spurted, then rolled into the cup, streaked with blood, like a fancy custard. He pressed gently to empty the tissue. Not a sound from the woman. He painted again with the iodine, then dressed the wound. He tapped the woman.

"All done. You keep it clean. Clean. Wash. Do you understand? With soap."

The woman nodded. She stood to go.

"I know," she said. "Soap. Thank you. You bring good medicine." She moved through the door ahead of him.

"Next," said Jerome Henderson. "Next."

They came and went all afternoon. He treated more boils, and scabies, and catarrh brought on by the hot tipis and cold weather. Two men and a woman were back with syphilis, and he gave them the arsphenamine, knowing while it might help, even cure them, they'd soon get it again, just as they couldn't stay out of the whiskey. It made Jerome ill to see the whites come up from Valentine and Cody and fan out with their rotgut liquor, against the regulations but with the Indian agent's wink, into the tribal communities. Some of it they adulterated with methanol, and then he'd have to treat the victims for the tremors and nerve damage, though he couldn't do much, not when the brain went dead. Now he vaccinated some children against the smallpox and tetanus, and with willow splints he set a broken carpus, result of a horse kick. He dispensed aspirin and turpinhydrate and codeine, and iodine pills against the goiter, and as much advice about cleanliness and sanitation as he could. Dysentery was nearly as big a problem as the flu, and he was getting low on the morphine pills that stopped the flux. But, without cleaning up the water supplies out there on the reservation proper, things'd continue bad. They sure didn't need any typhoid here, too, but he bet that'd be next.

At five, the hall and bedroom sat empty. Jerome rubbed his neck while clearing up the room. What day was it, anyway? Not that it mattered, except Sundays when the one preacher in town had a nondenominational service. He'd been raised staunch Roman Catholic, and he still believed, mostly, even if practicing a little medicine had convinced Jerome that some doctrines didn't fit reality too snugly. Edna, now, had been raised in that Methodist parsonage, but she said she'd convert if he asked her. Right now, what Jerome wanted to ask her was if there was coffee on the stove.

There was, but Edna wasn't in the kitchen. He found her upstairs, in their bedroom, turning one of his shirt collars.

"They gone?" she asked.

"Yes, poor devils. And that was just the ordinary stuff. I've got to go over to the quarantine now."

"You've got blood on your shirt again," she said. "Can't you wear the apron?"

"I will."

Jerome knew Edna felt pouty because all either of them seemed to do was work. She was especially touchy about the laundry, since even with the squaw who came to help, Edna had to supervise and heat the water, and there wasn't anyplace except the dining room to hang things to dry, not in this weather. Jerome finished his coffee.

"I'll take a quick look at the quarantine, then come right back."

Edna flashed him a nod and a smile before going back to her mending. She heard him clomp down the steps and stop for his overcoat before she heard the front door close. Yes, she'd try to tell him tonight, if he ever got finished with these Indians. She knew what he'd do now. Go into the old rooming house where all the influenza cases were quarantined and expose himself to the germs. Bend over to touch and take the temperature of them all, and give them the aspirin and make sure Mrs. Jackson, the preacher's wife, was giving them plenty of fluids, and he'd worry himself sick about the ones he knew wouldn't make it. They'd buried three last week, two old men and a six-year-old girl. Not exactly buried, though. Hacked a hole in the ground was more like it, as if planting a seed that would never grow. Still, Jerome was that way, and she loved him, so she'd just have to put up with his life. It was time to fix supper anyway, and after that they could sit and read and talk and go to bed, and then she'd tell him she was in the family way.

Years later, Edna often told the tale of how it didn't happen that way that night. Her civilized friends would utter mock-horrified gasps and oh-my-dear-please titters, although Edna told it out of a fierce grasp of the past and the way they'd been.

They'd hardly finished supper. The remains of the venison steaks, boiled potatoes, and dried corn still sat on the table while the coffeepot bubbled on the kerosene range. Jerome related a success with an influenza patient, while Edna thought about a hot bath with perfumed salts, and then her confession and some sweet lovemaking. Heavens! How she did enjoy that, especially in the down-quilted bed on a cold night, with the stars bright as beads, the windows frosted with their deep breathing, and the snow locked out. At such times, White River didn't seem so bad. Or even now, when Jerome's hand lay on hers, and they fell silent, listening to the winter wind squeak around the house, and the coffeepot sing. Afterward, she'd often asked who heard the other sounds first? The clank of the buckboard and the horses' snorting, then the running, hard footsteps, and the frenzied pounding on the door?

No matter. Jerome went. She heard an Indian's guttural staccato sounds, and Jerome replying, "Yes, yes, let me get my things, yes, stay here." Edna felt the chill from the hallway. She rose, for some reason clutching herself around the chest. Jerome appeared in the doorway.

"Darling, sorry, but a woman's got bad birthing trouble. I've got to go. Don't know how long I'll be."

He already wore his heavy coat and boots. He carried his medical bag and his gloves. A scarf wound around his neck, beneath the wide-brimmed felt hat that dwarfed his face.

"I'll come, too. I can help," Edna heard herself say. What on earth possessed her?

Jerome stared, then nodded. She could help, he knew. There'd be people there she could keep away, and in the matter of anatomy and bloody details she'd shown significant intestinal fortitude. He half-suspected she had some Indian in her. Nobody really knew her parentage. Besides, living at the preacher's farm she'd seen plenty of birthing, albeit among the lower animals.

"All right, hurry. Dress warm. We're in the wagon."

Neither Edna nor Jerome exactly recalled the journey out. The snow wasn't deep, thank God, no more than two inches, and the half-moon cast plenty of light. But the wind cut through even their heavy wool coats and the scarves they tied over their faces, so that their noses and lips numbed. The Indian man sat hunched on the driver's board, urging his ponies into a jolting trot, saying not a thing. He wore a thin buckskin coat and a round, black hat with an eagle feather stuck in the band. In the moonlight his face looked sculpted of red granite. They pounded south along the main road, then cut off on an eastward trail. Jerome could make out the ruts of the man's trip into town and thought, This must be serious. Usually their granny-women delivered the babies. He hoped his bag had what he might need.

He looked over at Edna. With one scarf tied down over her winter bonnet and under her chin and the other around her face she looked like a highwayman with a toothache. Frost coated the scarf at her mouth and nose. Her gloved hands were up under her armpits, and she stamped her feet to keep feeling in them. But she hadn't complained at all. Jerome peered ahead for some sign of life. The man hadn't said how far he'd come, but from the look of his ponies, it hadn't been too far. If it'd been a long way east he'd have fetched the saw-bones in Hidden Timber, though that drunken old ex-cavalry doctor wasn't good for much more than psoriasis and the occasional amputation. Jerome caught a whiff of wood smoke. The Indian was driving the ponies southward again, now, on a smaller trail, probably toward the Keya Paha River. He estimated they drove another ten minutes before he saw a light up ahead, and in another five they were there. He nudged Edna.

"Lucky. He's a cabin Indian."

She mumbled something through the scarf, but he only caught the words "who's lucky," before the Indian was lifting her down, and he was off the buckboard himself, headed toward the cottonwood-log cabin. Just inside the door, he and Edna both recoiled. The one room reeked of sweat and blood and coal oil and wood smoke. A roaring fire in the hearth made it feel like the steam baths at the Omaha YMCA, and Jerome felt his own sweat start. The crowd and noise oppressed him. Three old Indian women kneeled by the birth pallet, and around them moved a female shaman sprinkling something from a buffalo horn. In one corner, by the fireplace, hunkered a young man, no doubt an elder son, and in the other, three small children and a teenage girl. The Indian who'd fetched them stationed himself like a statue against the closed door. Jerome had a fleeting picture of how it would have been fifty years ago, the laboring woman in the birth tipi attended only by the old wives, and if the birth was difficult, a transverse lie or a breech, the slow death and the corpse up in the trees in the Lakota Sioux way. But these people were half-white in their ways, too often the bad half. Jerome saw that Edna had stripped off her coat, scarves and bonnet.

"Oh, my God, oh, my God," she was saying. "Jerome, Jerome." He looked at the rude pallet and then he was throwing off his things, too, and shouting at the Indian who must be the father, "Get them out. Get them out, all out now, except you and the children. Get them out." He shouted like a madman and flapped his arms. The sheer sight of it likely galvanized the Indians, this shortish white man in his whiteman's suit and little face-hair moustache and eyeglasses, screaming and making herding gestures. The Indian man started to shout, too, and he and Jerome and Edna began pushing people out into the cold. They went, except for the female shaman who waved her buffalo horn and talisman stick and shrieked in Lakota at the father, probably some kind of curse, and braced herself against the doorjamb.

"For Christ's sake, let her stay," Jerome hollered, motioning toward the corner where the son had been. He noticed the teenage girl comforting the young ones and, from the corner of his eye, saw the father drinking from a stoneware jug. He whiffed the pungent rotgut smell. But the overpowering smell now was blood and fear, and for the first time he heard the woman's moans, low and weak, like a bass fiddle string plucked and sustained.

"Edna, some hot water, and find some rags. We've got to clean her up and get that baby out. Edna!"

Jerome saw his wife start, shudder, then rip her eyes away from the laboring Indian woman and hurry to the cookstove. He looked more closely at the squaw. Not a pretty sight. The woman had bled a lot after the sack burst, he saw, onto the blankets folded beneath her, and she could barely keep her squatting position. She rocked, moaning, her face, her braids, slick with sweat. He wondered at her age. If that boy was eighteen, she could be anywhere from thirty to forty-five, depending on when she'd been given away, which depended on her dowry. She wasn't a pretty woman, particularly not now, with a prominent nose and puffy cheeks and a blocky body. Hard to give away. He went to her, squatted, and put his hands on her shoulders.

"I'm Dr. Henderson. From White River. Come to help. Please, now, lie down. I can help better if you do. Please now, lie down. We have to get the baby out."

The woman rocked on, her eyes glazed and unfocused. She didn't seem to see him. A contraction seized the woman, but weakly. He heard the moans take on a melody. Her birth song? Death song?

He pushed her back gently and felt the counterforce.

"Please, now. You must lie down. I will help. You must lie down so I can take the baby."

"Doctor, can I help?"

Jerome turned to see the teenage girl.

"Is this your mother?"

"Yes."

The girl spoke well. Must be good in the Bureau school.

"Please tell her she must lie down so I can help. We don't want her to die, or the baby."

The girl kneeled by her mother's side. Jerome heard her whispering in Lakota. A stream of words. The woman's eyes cleared and came up to meet Jerome's. More words. Then the woman nodded and, with the girl's help, collapsed back on the pallet. The girl held her mother's hand and kept speaking to her.

Jerome spread the woman's legs and saw the trouble. The baby was breech, one foot in the vaginal canal, which meant the baby was twisted. Trouble on trouble, and he was no expert at this. Another contraction came.

"Jerry?"

Edna held a pan of hot water. He opened his bag for the strong naphtha soap, then washed quickly. No gloves. He'd have to feel this. He poured a weak solution of perchloride of mercury over his hands. He reached for the ammonia ampule. Might help her contract. She was too weak.

"Edna?"

She took the ampule and snapped it under the woman's nostrils. The woman coughed, shook, but perked up.

"Do that whenever she seems to flag," he told Edna and, rolling up his shirt sleeves, bent to his work.

Telling the story later, Edna could see it all, even if she couldn't frame the words just right. But she had it all as clear as when it happened, and she'd not since been as proud of Jerry, despite the great things he'd done. She saw herself kneeling at the woman's head, across from the girl. Saw herself with the ampules and, when Jerry told her, with the bite stick for the woman's mouth, when Jerry took the scalpel and cut down on the vagina to widen the opening. "Major episiotomy," he said. The woman's teeth crunched on the stick and a low sound escaped her, but nothing more. Edna remembered the woman's husband turning away in his corner to drink the whiskey.

"Edna, if the pain gets too bad and she starts to thrash, you hold this over her nose and put just a few drops on it. Not much. I want her awake to help."

Jerome had handed her the ether mask and the can. Then he was smearing his right hand and forearm with sterile petroleum jelly. His crimped hand disappeared into the woman.

"My God, that's good. She's dilated to beat the band, and she's not bleeding much. But I need contractions."

"I'll do it," the girl said, taking the ampules from Edna. The woman stiffened at the ammonia.

"I've got the baby," Jerome said. They could see his hand moving inside the woman's belly.

"Tell her to help me, to push," Jerome told the girl. Edna watched the girl speak to the woman, watched her belly ripple and her lips whiten with the effort.

"It's turning, thank God, it's turning," Jerome said. He knelt between the woman's legs, head off to the side, his arm up in her like Edna had seen the preacher do with cows. She felt a sudden twinge of nausea. Blood trickled down Jerry's arm.

"Turning, turning, by God, there, there, look, by God," and he withdrew his hand. Edna peeked. Was that its head, that wrinkled black thing? The girl looked, too, unflinching at her mother's vagina, swollen, open, bleeding.

"Now, she's got to help," Jerome hollered. "Got to, or we'll have to cut her open. Cut her open like a hog. Tell her that. Tell her we don't want that. Tell her we need her strength."

The girl spoke louder to her mother, pulling on one of her braids. The Indian man came to look over Edna's shoulder, grunted, and went back to his corner and whiskey.

"The ampules," Jerry told Edna, and she snapped another under the woman's nose, and then Jerry leaned over the woman and slapped her hard across the mouth. The woman's eyes flew open.

"Shove, goddam it," he swore. "Push or you'll die and the baby will, too. Shove!" And he hit her again. The girl's eyes widened in shock, then narrowed as she understood. Now the woman labored in earnest, her eyes angry, her mouth open, the bite stick pushed aside, and her cries of terror and fear and pain echoing in the smoky, smelly cabin. Jerome heard the shaman commence a drum-like chant. Boom-thud-boom-thud.

"Coming, here it comes. Coming," exclaimed Jerry, and Edna saw him reach again into the woman, this time with the big spoon forceps she'd boiled, and then the baby's head appeared out of the woman in the forceps, and Jerry gently removed them. Edna saw the creases the forceps left on the wrinkled, copper-and-black skull. Jerry had the baby's shoulders now, and with a tug the buttocks and legs appeared, trailing the umbilical cord. Jerry's forefinger went to the infant's mouth, pried it open and swiped out mucus. He blew frantically in it, and with a cotton swab cleared out the nose. He turned the baby upside down. The smacks rang through the cabin. One of the smaller children started to wail, and then Edna and the rest heard the thin cry of the newborn, and Jerry smiled.

"Look at that," he said, holding the baby head-up. "Just look at that, will you, a little girl, and alive as can be." The Indian man grunted again. The girl held her mother's head up to see, but Edna detected no reaction. Jerry handed up the baby.

"Edna, wash her off, will you, and find something to wrap her in."

Edna did, with the girl's help, while Jerry cut the umbilicus now with the surgical scissors, then quickly sutured the stem. He dabbed carbolic acid on the sutures. Then he delivered the placenta and stitched up the woman, carefully washing her and using the antiseptic. The girl brought him a clean rag for a sanitary napkin. He soaked the carbolic into it and placed it on the woman, who now lay still as if she were dead, except for the steady heaving of her chest. The infant squirmed in Edna's arms.

"Give her the baby," Jerome said, and Edna saw how weary he looked now, standing in the room's center, the color drained from his face, his hands trembling. Old, Lord, he looked almost old, lots older than twenty-four.

"You can let them in, now," Jerome said. The girl jabbered to the father, who threw open the door. The women boiled in first, to crowd around the pallet, and the shaman danced over, still chanting.

"Thank you, Doctor. You saved both lives," the girl said.

"You helped," Jerry told her. "And we were lucky. You tell your mother to keep clean, and take care of the baby. And not to have any more for a while. No intercourse, no braves, for two months. You understand? No men. Will you tell her that?"

Edna noticed the girl's mouth tighten, and her dark eyes narrow. She was pretty in a way, this Indian girl. Slim, with a longer face than most Sioux, but with their born-in dignified bearing.

"She didn't want more, Doctor. But . . . but . . ." The girl stopped.

"I see," Jerome said, looking at the father, standing expressionless in the corner. "Then tell her no men for *six* months. Doctor's orders. And tell her to come see me. We can talk about *not* having babies."

Edna stiffened. Jerry was Catholic. He'd never mentioned, what was the ten-dollar word, *contraception,* to her, and here she was, probably pregnant, and not much older than this girl.

"I never want babies," the girl suddenly blurted out. "Never." She shook her long black braids violently.

"You'll get over that," Jerry said, "but at your age, if you mean it, come see me. I'll introduce you to Margaret Sanger." He looked square at Edna. "Darling, let's go home."

The girl called in Lakota to her father. He nodded, and she called again. The son appeared from outside and motioned that they were to come. Jerome took a last look at the woman, who seemed to be sleeping propped up against a squaw, the infant pulling at her breast. He shrugged into his coat and helped Edna with hers. Then they were in the cold, on the buckboard. The moon had nearly set, but the wind had laid, too. They rode with arms around each other. Their house felt deliciously warm. Edna forsook her bath, settling for a warm wash-up. When she crawled beneath the comforter, Jerome was half-asleep. Another day for her surprise. But she itched with a question.

"Jerry," she asked, "why did you mention that birth-control woman? I thought you liked babies, and big families."

He smiled, his eyes half open.

"I do for us. For people who want them, can afford them."

"And the Indians?"

"You saw. The way they're kept, they're like brutes in a breeding ground."

"Come now. Maybe not like us, but they're people, too, aren't they?"

But she saw he was fast asleep.

# The Novice Writer
# Explores Cartography

Aping Yeats, I've sought my theme in vain. Too many times.
Yet the story urges itself. It isn't a question of elements. I have
those. There is a boy whose sweat rancors the funeral-chapel
limousine on both occasions. There is the town both times, a
Norman Rockwell town, with wide streets and open faces on
the passers-by. There is both times the cemetery, surrounded
by corn fields, a small green square set in the gold. Other elements, too. Flowers. Relatives. Weather.

What's missing is the theme. It can't simply be death. Nor
maturation. Nor any other off-the-shelf catchall. It is, I guess,
something like the coordinates of grief. But how to render
that? How explain just what it is that this boy becoming man
felt . . .

It is his father in the long metal box. His father dead from a hole somewhere in his intestines. His father for whom he prayed and whom he believed was stronger than the strongest sickness. His father who taught him how to bunt, to read books, to cry only when it hurt too much. They lower the metal box. The straps creak. The wind blows. The corn's leaves and husks rub. The corn makes the sound kids make when they put a leaf between their thumbs and hiss through it. The metal box is down. A stranger says the prayers. His mother, whom he should hold, is hugged by her mother. He stands to the side, awkward, feeling that he is not here, that the wind will blow all this away like it blew the heat shimmers from the metal box. No townspeople are there. His father left this place long ago. Only his name, the name of his father's father and of what will be the boy's children persists, etched into the granite brought from the Rockies by the Union Pacific . . .

Is that grief? Rendered grief? By art's standards it is only an emotional moment in the psyche. Dragged out this way its sentimentalism shows. That, of course, one day might be the armature of something sturdy, but today it is only a stark, one-dimensional wire. So, return to metaphor. Meridians of grief, I suggested. Meridians are lines of cartography. They form great circles around the earth, passing through the poles. They show location. The meridian of Greenwich also determines time. Meridians are where and when . . .

Another time. Another metal box. His mother is inside. The heat waves rise again. A different stranger drones on about being unafraid in the valley of death. The boy is not afraid. He is tired and angry. He has come with the box on the Union Pacific, sitting up all night and day, watching for the hills to flatten and the corn to begin. The men at the depot touched the box gingerly, respectfully, as though it contained a powerful medicine. But it held only remains. The tissues are full of alcohol and barbiturates, but they are only remains. His mother's mother cries again that the boy's mother was not that kind of woman. The wind again clacks the corn. Again he feels awkward, but mostly angry. His mother's husband, not his father, is here. He's drunk and sobs in stagey grief. The granite will bear his name . . .

So. There the boy is set in another location and in an idea of time. But what the boy felt, apparently, is nothing. And all the grief, the theme, is retrospective. That raises an interesting question: If the boy felt nothing then, how can I make him feel something now? That's not a question for art, of course, which is concerned with effect, not process. Maybe the answer is that he doesn't need to feel anything now, but only needs to seem as if he had felt something. Is texture all? . . .

In the hospital the doctors said his father was getting well. Antibiotics were wonderful. The hole in his guts had poisoned him, but the drugs would fix that. They were so sure that they let the boy visit. Let him watch his father pick at the covers with long, fielder's-glove fingers. Let him hear his father shout, "Goddam it! Get out of the flowers, you're squashing the blossoms, Goddam it!" His father had lucid moments, too. He asked the boy how school was going, how the White Sox were doing, and if he was helping his mother. The doctors were so sure they told the boy's mother to let him go out on Friday night, and when he came home from the movie his mother's mother folded him into her big arms and told him. Then she cried, and he felt that somehow it was all his fault. That if he had not gone out, not booted a ground ball, not been at all, he would not then be falling fast through darkness . . .

This then, you see, is as recorded now. To try for more precise texture—how strong the grandmother's arms were, what

scent she wore, how late they stayed up, how the funeral plans were made, how much the adults drank—could be interesting. But art has to be edited, compressed, doesn't it, so the theme stands clear? Some things have to go. Like the fact that these characters undoubtedly would have recalled the father's joke that he was so poor he'd have a one-car funeral. Surely, too, the mother would have wept and told the boy he'd have to be the man now. He would agree, of course, and have no idea what she meant. But let those go. Pursue the theme, the prevailing emotional valences. Who and why and how the weather was . . .

When the front and rear doors of the apartment were open, the icy wind poured in like water. "The Hawk" they call that wind in Chicago. Leaving, the coroner had left the front door open. The rear door was open because the boy's stepfather had stumbled out that way to call the police when he'd awakened and found dead beside him, spittle drooling from her mouth, the boy's naked mother. Neighbors stole appliances and gadgets while he was gone. The policeman said the stepfather had to mumble his message several times because he was too drunk to talk straight. Her pubic hair was blonde. It was gummy, the coroner reported. Her heart had stopped, the coroner said, because of bourbon and phenobarbital. She was at the mortician's when the boy arrived. He chose her metal box, as gold as he could get. He brought with him her burial clothes. A white linen dress and black-bead jewelry. Her gold-blonde hair he had swept back in soft curls. He insisted she wear shoes. When he returned to the apartment the rear door was still open. The stepfather sat in his father's red leather chair, drinking vodka. He smelled because he had beshit himself. The boy did not let the stepfather sit beside him on the train taking the box west. When he cried he did it alone. He thought over and over about how six hours before she died she had called and said, "Come get me! I've had enough." Not long after the funeral the boy married . . .

Now, does that go far enough? Grief's coordinates, like Rand McNally's, intersect at many places. I suppose those junctions constitute theme. The trouble is, there are so many intersections. They form a vast grid of feelings, and so when you approach a junction you can feel all along it, in all directions, like putting your hand on a harp and plucking just one string. Infinite harmonic vibrations. Seeking the theme is seeking the intersection of the main emotions . . .

The last time the weather was cold. The corn was stubble. Frost held on the cemetery's stiff brown grass. The grass crunched when the boy walked on it. He recalled Whitman: the uncut hair of graves. At the first grave he ran his fingers over his name, cut deep against the harsh climate. He put a red mum in the bronze-painted urn. Then he walked to the second grave. He did not look at the name that was not his. He tried to stare through the earth but saw only the stiff brown grass. He put a white mum in the urn. He walked a hundred feet, turned and looked back. He sighted along the line between himself and the two graves. If continued, it would go around the world, then curve into space as part of the celestial sphere, of the great circle. It would pass through everyone standing on its path before coming back through him and the graves. It was, he saw, a meridian, and its compass point would never change. He stood for several minutes, feeling its intersections. Then he drove home over a different line to his wife and children . . .

You see how vexing this theme seeking is? Do I have it? Or have I only come at another time in vain? Art is tricky. Grids, intersections, junctions, meridians of grief all only approximate what I felt. Perhaps approximations is the theme. Still, one must keep seeking. I can always start again in Yeats's foul rag-and-bone shop of the heart. I can always repeat to myself the fundamental elements: that I still weep because I miss them and because I could not save them and because I cannot say so well enough.

# Moriarty's True Colors

Moriarty pressed his nose against the storm door's glass. He kept his hips slightly thrust back so his Levis wouldn't touch the panes and cool his erection. Next to him, standing on small white hind feet, was Louie, their black-and-white cat. Louie, too, stared out at the gray, rainy morning. Across the street, crouched beneath a bush, his girl friend howled. Louie's erection, if he had one, was hidden up in his body. On Moriarty's other side stood Tashi. Tashi, Moriarty thought, was the horniest Lhasa Apso in America, and certainly one of the biggest. Low groans issued from his bearded visage, like temple chants. Tashi lusted for his mother, a block away, just into heat again. The dog's testicles bulged under long, silky black fur. Moriarty wondered if his fellow lusters felt as ignoble as he, but of course they did not. They didn't have to admit animality. They were animals.

"Still raining?" Moriarty's wife asked.

"Yes."

He heard her pen return to the letter. A love letter. Last winter's lover, now far away. Moriarty's excitement subsided. He'd not get out this afternoon, not find his love, his lover.

"Meeeeee-owwwww," moaned Louie.

Tashi growled, uttered a stifled little bark.

"Oh, God! Those animals!" his wife said. "Just let them out. With any luck they'll be run over."

Moriarty turned from the door. His right foot thrust Louie back. A hard look drove Tashi back toward the kitchen table.

"They're just horny," he said. She threw cold eyes, then scratched out a phrase. He sat at the table. They were comfortable with one another. They'd reached that stage at which they still loved one another, but didn't like one another. He watched her pen form the blue words. Once he had vowed never to write love letters. Say it with flowers, say it with drink, but never, never say it with ink. Something perverse happened, though. Now he could write love letters much easier than love.

"Where did we go wrong?" Moriarty asked. Louie leaped onto the chair beside him, mewling. He pushed him off. The cat's paws thumped the worn linoleum.

"We? You started it."

"No," he said. "You started it. I just continued it. In between Victor and what's his name."

She scratched out another phrase. A draft. She would perfect it.

"Between Victor and Franz were fifteen years," she said. "And three kids and you."

Tashi sidled up to rest his head on Moriarty's lap. Fair enough. He knew his wife could add: *And your several conquests.*

"Abstinence makes the heart grow fonder?"

She managed a smile.

"I didn't abstain from you. Did you abstain from anybody, fond of them or not?"

"Love's different, right? Now you're in love."

"Yes. Aren't you?"

He didn't know.

"Aren't you? Or has it all been some time-release revenge?" She held the pen between her hands as if she would break it.

"I still love you," he said. It felt half-true, like a promise to a wheedling child.

She looked again at the paper. A thin howl came from outside. Tashi's head swiveled toward the door. Louie stood there again, against the glass, head cocked. Tashi moved toward the cat. The pen moved again. Moriarty felt each stroke.

"Do you love him?" he asked. "Actually love him?"

"I think so."

"Is that what you're writing?"

"Part of it. He's thousands of miles away." Tashi sniffed Louie. The cat showed teeth when Tashi tried to mount him. A hiss, a quick box to the snout, and the dog was off. Safe for now, Louie darted for his pillow.

"Animals," he said.

"What's the difference?" she asked.

"I still love you. I do. Only we're different. Everything is."

"You're thinking about the baby, aren't you?"

Now Tashi pawed at the door, claws rasping on the glass. Moriarty saw that sunlight had come to play on the rain, painting the drops yellow as lemons. Moriarty thought he could see another color in the canine skull, a pulsating red glow. Instinct's color? What then was reason's color? The humanizing color? But wasn't instinct also human? Maybe all the somatic, genetic, experiential essences were colorless. If so, then what color was he? Or she? Tashi, discouraged, dropped to lie on the entrance mat.

"Aren't you?" she said again.

"Yes. It started to get different then."

She looked again at the letter. Her pen stabbed an i's dot. Inside her skull would be what color, he wondered. Anger's orange? Sorrow's bruise-purple? Something pastel, maybe, between love and hate. Love and hate for him, for them, for herself, for, perhaps, even the baby now become a child.

"I'm sorry," he said.

"I'm not." The pen came up to point at Moriarty's eyes. "Look at him. Really look, like when he comes off the bus. He's splendid. Like a little god."

"Funny, that's what the Mexicans called the magic mushroom."

She stared through him.

"Don't be cynical. He's healthy."

"I meant it," Moriarty said. "He's magic, too."

She returned the pen to the paper. The scratching irritated Moriarty's ears. He remembered his shock when she told him there would be another. Do you want it? Yes. Are you sure? It's alive, it's mine. His shrug. His nine-month white-red resentment. Then the summer solstice, the baby lying sideways, emergency surgery during a thunderstorm that cut the electricity, a boy baby born in generator light when the sun was at the full. Now he loved the boy, but she loved him more. Moriarty hoped it was enough to fill her where her lover had been, where he had once been.

"Why?" he asked. "Why did you have him?"

She held the pen again like a stick to be broken.

"Which?" she asked. "Doesn't matter, does it?"

Moriarty turned to see the sunlight and prismatic rain drops.

"To keep you," she said then. "Because I loved you. An old trick that lost its magic." She laid the pen on her letter. He could feel her slowed respiration. He could feel her glowing amber like the afternoon light.

"Yes," he said. He thought, now my son cries when anything, a plastic soldier, is hurt.

"Yes," he said again.

She stood, holding her letter and pen.

"I'm going to lie down."

Her passing disturbed Louie. The cat stretched, pushed his paws out like furry quatrefoils. Louie arched his way to stand beside Tashi, who roused himself. Cat and dog, they stood to stare out. A lemon drop snailing down the door caught the cat's eye. He mewled. The bearded dog groaned, high and strangled. The cat's tail switched, its end curled like a field-hockey stick. Moriarty sighed and went to stand between them.

The light seemed to flow in the rain, to coat the basketball goal, driveway, street, horizon. Soon the child, his son, would step from the bus into the golden puddles. Perhaps he, too, would glow, perhaps roseate. Soon it would be solstice time again. Heat time. Peasants would throw tokens of their troubles into bonfires, eat magic mushrooms, take the little god into themselves to conceive visions of what's beyond: reds, blues, yellows, oranges, purples, all twirly cornucopias melding the spectrum of perception. So, what color would Moriarty and his wife glow? Animal and human? Old and young?

Moriarty pulled hard on the door handle.

"Go on," he said. "Go!"

Tashi bounded through, his tail up, water and light shedding from his fur. Louie darted like a leopard cleaving soaked Serengeti sawgrass. Moriarty watched them dash their separate ways to love, splashing across the street along different paths.

Then he turned, irrationally aroused, and started for the bedroom, which he recalled she had done all in white, very long ago.

# Moriarty's Spells

Moriarty knew he had bad spells. Like when he'd go to Mass on one of those infrequent Sundays and in the new way, the priest or deacon or frocked layperson would tell him to turn to the stranger next to him and exchange the kiss or hand-shake of peace. When a spell came on, Moriarty would go red, and he'd turn and snarl, "Go fuck yourself for peace." If his auditor, and he always sat next to women, looked stricken enough, Moriarty would bolt from the pew with a string of oaths and head shakes, babbling that he had Tourette's syn-drome, but sometimes when his fellow communicant stood her ground, insisting on the rite, Moriarty would begin to cry and beg her forgiveness. A few times that tactic got him laid, but casual church sex did little to excise his conviction that his spells, his bad Mass behavior, really came from a trinity, a triangulation of three women: his ex-wife, his present wife, and a stockbroker's wife.

Moriarty figured, too, that some, maybe most, of being triangulated was his fault. He'd made himself a target by running his life as if it were an obstacle course with him as the steeplechase master. At least, that's what the stockbroker's wife, Sandra, had told him. Moriarty tended to believe her, although he didn't know just why.

"Your problem, Thomas," she said, "is that you think of 'women' and not the individual woman. You *want* me as an obstacle, a hurdle you can't jump, so you'll fall down and bruise yourself and regret everything ever afterwards. Now, if I want a man, I want him not as an emblem but as an individual who can connect to me, heart or mind. I'll take either."

Of course, Moriarty rationalized, she'd been buck naked when she said that, and he hoped fulfilled. At least she was dribbling. And he certainly was deflated. But Sandra's analysis bothered him and cast him into a spell.

"And now, please, exchange the kiss or handshake of peace." Moriarty heard the words as if freshly spoken, but they were in his head. Which head was in the kitchen of his ex-wife, where he'd taken many a meal, many a drink, and many a slap in the latter days of their dissolution.

"One of the things that was wrong," his ex-wife was saying through the imagined priest's command, "is that there was no genuine intimacy between us. I wanted hugs. I wanted kisses. A pat on the shoulder. Hell, when I had the kids and was lying there sore and exhausted you wouldn't even peck my forehead."

Moriarty thought: What you wanted was for me to kiss your sore, exhausted ass. But what he said was, "Sarah, I often kissed you, and we were often intimate. That didn't save the marriage, did it?"

"You didn't mean it," Sarah said. "I was just a thing to you."

With that, she thrust the box of Moriarty's mementoes toward him, the last he'd get from their home of nineteen years. His high-school newspapers, his army discharge, an old ball glove, several dozen snapshots, his old calendars holding runic reminders of what had been ("Dinner at O'Malleys," "Pick up kids at school for shots," "Dentist today"), and atop it all, his huge family Bible.

"Thanks," he said, turning for the door. "I'll call you."

"Call me what?" she asked. "For what?" Yet she held her cheek toward him for a kiss. Moriarty brushed the smooth surface with his lips, eyes closed, thinking how like an ass it was, and how like an ass he was. So much he felt a spell coming on. He always did when he had to go home.

"Honey, I'm home," Moriarty trilled coming in the condo's entryway. He thought he sounded like a funny 1960s TV husband-father. Ward Cleaver? But Kimberley—oh, how glad he was that she hadn't another S-name—doubtless didn't recognize it as such. Anything before 1971, when Kim was five, lay on her brain map as terra incognita. Her comment about anything Moriarty brought down from the great peaks of his overwhelming age, for he'd achieved forty-seven years, was invariably, "What's that gotta do with *me*?" Still, she was a sweet and willing thing, even if she didn't recognize that the names of the Mutant Teenage Ninja Turtles had historical overtones. But she was what he'd bought, or more accurately, he was what she'd bought, the teacher she'd had a crush on, slept with, found vulnerable, and married.

"Honey? Oh, you're so late. The pizza already came. You told me six-thirty. But you can zap a piece."

Kimberley's kiss fell on Moriarty's forehead like rose-scented crayon. On the butcher-block table rested the Domino's pepperoni special, or its three remaining pieces. And a rose-scented iced-tea glass. And Moriarty's Notre Dame college mug, unfilled until he filled it with whatever cheap beer he could afford after the settlement with Sarah.

"Beer's in the fridge. Got to take my run. Bye!"

This kiss fell on Moriarty's cheek like a leech. He could feel the blood being sucked. God, she ran every evening. Forty-five minutes. Came in dripping with female sweat. Showered. Watched the nine-o'clock *thirtysomething* equivalent. Watched ten o'clock news. Watched *A Current Affair,* once saying she just couldn't understand how any woman could poison her husband, cut him up, store his pieces in the freezer, putting one out a week for the garbage truck until he was all gone. Actually, Moriarty was glad she couldn't fathom that. Then she'd go to bed to read Janet Dailey. Always smelled sweet when he came at last to bed.

If he wasn't too drunk or tired or bored, they'd make love. Whatever, she always cuddled. Kissed his shoulder. Scratched his back. Never snored. And Moriarty would doze with the church scenes, the divorce scenes, the banal-life scenes playing like a triple feature in his mind until he'd wake up at the drinker's hour and wonder who he was with until he remembered it wasn't the afternoon. He wasn't with Sandra, he wasn't with Sarah. It was he and Kimberley. Newlyweds at eight months, and often enough he'd cry until she'd hear and nuzzle his back and stroke his forehead. After that, he'd feel for the moment useful and alive, like the steeplechase hadn't all been for nought. Unless it was particularly bad. Then he'd have a spell. As now, when after a lukewarm shower, he put himself into the guest bedroom, with Kim safe asleep in their bed wrapped in the righteousness of physical weariness, and Moriarty told off some beads of his life.

"I love you, Tom," he heard Sarah say from years ago. "I do. And our children love you, but we can't live with the drinking, the abuse. I can't live with the other women. Please, Tom, please."

For a moment, Moriarty struggled to talk with that memory, formulating his defenses, his confessions, mumbling them like prayers before he again realized he could not reason with, apologize to, a memory.

He evoked another bead.

"Oh, God, oh, God, ooooooh, Lord, Tom, you are deprived, oooooohhh, my." Moriarty now saw himself with Sandra their first time, after they'd met at the party for the visiting pianist, after Moriarty had taken to living in a small, white apartment furnished with thrift-store relics, including the creaky hotel bed on which he had spread Sandra and Sandra spread him. He heard himself breathe the fateful words, "I love you," and again heard Sandra: "No, you don't, but we are good together, and I'll take that. Besides, you can't afford another marriage and I can't afford a divorce."

Moriarty's fleshy hand grasped at this bead, moving through the bedroom's dark air toward this bidden image. But his fingers closed only on that air, not on the ghostly auras of the long affair that had gotten him through the divorce and into the new marriage, and now—Jesus, *now* how much he wanted to talk with Sandra—well, *now* had sustained Moriarty's illusion that there was something to live for. He dropped his hand to mind another bead.

"Thomas Moriarty, I swear you're so silly. Age doesn't mean anything. So, just stop acting like a fool and do it to me and we can get married if you want. My daddy doesn't care. He's been married three times so he knows you can just keep trying until you get it right." Kim, his Kim, encountered in his class on Romantic poetry and prose, taken because she needed the credit to at last graduate after years of travel and paternal indulgence, and he teaching it because he wanted to prove to his innocent students that Blake was full of shit, that the path of excess led to the loony bin, not the palace of wisdom. Kim, his pretty Kim, who after a few coffees and some war stories decided why the hell not with Moriarty, he of course knowing that for her there was always the safety hatch of youth and knowing that his was forever closed to the kind of illusions that blew through her from ear to ear. But she was sweet and had a wealthy father with whom Moriarty could exchange false protestations of conservatism in exchange for the old man's blessing, and perhaps in time, an annuity. So they had married, honeymooned in Manzanillo at a friend of Daddy's, and returned to live in Kim's condo.

Beads. Too many beads. Moriarty turned to press himself against the waffled mattress. He counted sins until he dozed.


"Professor! Professor!" Moriarty, although awake and speaking, did not immediately hear the call. Then he located the intruder, an owlish, red-haired graduate student of immense ass-paining ability who commuted each morning from a bedroom suburb to harass poor working folk like Moriarty.

"Professor?"

"Uh, yes, Mr. Potts?"

"Dr. Moriarty, what you say about Joyce and time and tradition may be right, but what about Heisenberg's principle of uncertainty? Applied here, doesn't it suggest that Leopold Bloom cannot be located by place, Dublin, and time, Bloomsday, simultaneously—and therefore the text is hopelessly corrupt? Meaningless?"

The class, especially graduate students, shifted in their seats. A few chuckled. *Épaté le professeur.* Moriarty felt the dull rage he usually associated with all those pre-dissolution arguments with Sarah. Her specialty, too, was applying abstract, irrelevant principles, like ethics, to personal relationships, a field entirely outside of ethics. Moriarty cleared his throat.

"Mr. Potts, in quantum mechanics the principle of uncertainty refers solely to the axiom that it is impossible to measure simultaneously and exactly two related quantities. For instance, the position and momentum of a particle. Now, *Ulysses* is a book, a collection of signs, that is intended to measure just such two quantities, by comparison *and* absolutely, namely, Leopold and Odysseus. Thus, your principle is false because Joyce has so disproved it and Heisenberg."

Potts' face began to flush, but Moriarty saw he was too far in to retreat.

"But, Professor," Potts said, preening for the females arrayed around him, "surely you don't dispute that a 'collection of signs,' as Derrida would say, means nothing and is therefore totally uncertain as to effect, intended or otherwise."

Moriarty's red rage now painted the room scarlet. He heard Sarah speaking in his brainpan—"surely, Thomas, you know I hate you for what you've done to me, I hate you, because now nothing is certain"—and Moriarty sighed. Why argue with such reasoning? Then, in the millisecond following the sigh and preceding his words, he saw the eyes in every skull before him widen, as if he, a Figure, could not sigh so, could not and should not admit distress.

"Shut the fuck up, Mr. Potts!" Moriarty shrieked. "Class dismissed." With that he was through the door, into the institutional beige hall, and headed down the staircase for his old Volkswagen. Hell, this was spring break day, and Potts would forget soon enough. And, this was Sandra's day at home.

"Moriarty, you just don't get it, do you?"

Sandra stood brushing her hair before the full-length mirror in which Moriarty could see her face, shoulders, breasts, and pantied bottom, and by straining, his own detumescent self on his side, like a Naked Majo, looking at her looking at him. Stroke, stroke, the imported boar's-hair brush glided through Sandra's radiant hair. Stroke, stroke; that was what he should have been doing, but it hadn't happened. He'd stayed limp as a banker's handshake. Sandra of give-me-mine-now-please hadn't tried very hard to cure him. Her hair, after all, wanted brushing.

"Get what?" Moriarty asked. He rolled onto his stomach, anticipating a frontal attack. Stroke, stroke, stroke.

"Women. A woman. You don't get us at all." Moriarty swiveled on his belly like a revolving spice tray to look at her directly. Stroke, stroke, stroke. "See, you think we're completely different from you, that we can't feel or think or act in any way like your stupid sex. Once you make that mistake, and all men do, nothing's permanent in the way of communication."

"Oh?"

"Oh."

"So? Pray tell me those cosmic similarities."

"OK. We are as aggressive, politic, insecure, bright, dumb, sensitive, and unfeeling as men. Like men we need the reassurance and honesty of our loves, our families, our worlds. We are not fragile. We are not dense. We react to those worlds the way we've been brought up in or otherwise conditioned by those worlds, and we constantly check our realities against all the lessons those worlds give us."

Stroke, stroke, stroke. Moriarty felt a headache coming on.

"Of course, there is a major difference, and it's not in plumbing or hormones or in what both men and women have to a fatal fare-the-well, romantic thinking."

"What is it?" Moriarty felt his testicles receding, the surest sign of an oncoming spell.

"Women can love. Men can only be loving."

"For Christ's sake," he blurted, "what's that mean? You sound like some of my half-assed philosophy colleagues, or this jerk student I've got who wants to make a physicist into a literary critic. Or best, the number three story in a supermarket tabloid."

Sandra turned to face him. God, she was beautiful, even shrugging into a sweat shirt. She wasn't smiling. More of a wise smirk. Or a vainglorious glower.

"It means that women can cast an umbrella of love. And under it can *choose* to permit, even encourage, mistakes, misbehaviors, follies, falsehoods, and yet still love what's under the umbrella. Man or woman or child."

"An umbrella," Moriarty said. He hoped the arch tone reached her. "And is this also for sunny weather? And what happens when it's folded up?"

"Sunny and rainy. And when a woman decides to fold it, she's gone. Forever. But your sex, well."

Moriarty felt his penis responding to what must be its own tiny brain's command to become a bit engorged.

"My sex is what? Only loving? What's wrong with that?"

Now Sandra did wear a wise smirk.

"Listen. And tell that thing to settle down. Listen. Love is absolute. Loving is relative. Got it? Good. And you can let yourself out. I'm going to sauna and shower."

By the time Sandra had whistled past the bed Moriarty could hardly find his parts to secrete back in his underwear.

For no good reason, Moriarty felt comfortable with Sarah when he had a truly bad spell like this, except when they were quarreling violently. Bad luck he counted it that most times he saw her they were either quarreling or quibbling about past quarrels. Sniping, Moriarty called it. Long- and short-range sniping with the deadly accuracy that only people who have lived together for a long time have. But now, he just might take his chances.

The house he'd worked tolerably hard to buy stood large and white before him. The hundred-pound doghouse he'd built years ago of scrap lumber and shingled with cast-off green Seal-Tabs looked almost as good. Solid. But, like his part of the house, empty. Sarah gave away his dog long ago. Moriarty stepped on the irregular flagstones leading to the back door as if they were the marked path through a minefield. He reminded himself to ring the bell as the divorce counselor told him. One of the few good pieces of advice that he'd gotten for two thousand or so dollars. That, and to think before he reacted to any deed or statement of his ex. Shit, there was that much wisdom in a Rosicrucian manual. He pushed the doorbell button.

Sarah wore jeans and, considering the kids, looked tidy in the stone-washed blue. He recognized the striped blouse. One of his old shirts, the tails tied in front. Straggles of brown hair escaped at her temples from the pull-back. She wore yellow Rubbermaid gloves.

"Hello," she said. "Come to help scrub floors?" She pulled the door farther open for him.

"No. I was just in the neighborhood. I just . . . are the kids here?"

"Tom, it's a school day. So, why aren't you in school?"

He smelled Pine-Sol and the acidic aroma of an orange peel. Their son, his namesake and now a point guard on the high-school team, loved oranges.

"Gave 'em a reading assignment. Maybe we could talk."

Sarah turned back toward the kitchen.

"Watch your feet. Talk about what? Why?"

"Us. Men and women. You know."

"Do you want a cup of coffee? It's stale, from this morning."

"Sure."

He remembered the old mug from a trip they'd made to San Francisco. A blue gull flew across the gray stoneware. The coffee tasted bitter.

"Us?" Sarah asked. She plunged the sponge mop into the bucket, splashing brown-green liquid on the lower cabinet fronts. She sat at the table, facing him. "There isn't any us. You made it that way. Remember?"

"I know, but . . ."

"Do you know what I did last night, Tom? After work and dinner? I dropped Tommy off at his friend Mike's, and I took Katy over to my mother's to watch a movie on her VCR, and then I went alone to the mall." Moriarty watched her eyes. Sarah was a cryer. This wasn't going well. She'd weep soon. Oh, a spell. "And I wandered it, Tom, like a bag lady, shop to shop, until I wound up in Taylor's, in the lingerie department."

He saw the tears congregating on her lower eyelids. How he hated that. For all their married life she'd turned on those tears to shame him or glorify her sensitivity or demonstrate the sort of martyrdom that wronged wives need in place of lost love. Or at least that's what his quarrelsome self said. But then she'd always said that it was his insensitivity to her, his callousness, his spells, his nettling tongue, that goaded her to the weeps.

"Lingerie? Sarah, are you dating?" Moriarty felt the dead jest fall cold into his cup. He saw the first tears fall toward hers.

"You listen to me . . . you listen, I just stood there, stood there watching young people and old people, fat people, pretty people, skinny people, plug-uglies, all kinds, but in couples . . . do you hear that? in couples! Buying underwear for the women. Because they loved them, do you hear that? Do you hear that?"

Sarah's head and shoulders shook now. Moriarty imagined those tears flung out of the brown eyes into a strobe, each droplet segmented by spectra, red and yellow and blue, each solid as a crystal, solid and shattering on the old gate-leg kitchen table.

"But, Sarah," he said, "buying a bra or a slip doesn't mean love. I mean . . ."

But she was on her feet, leaning across the table, shaking her finger in his face.

"You son-of-a-bitch, that's the life I have now because of you, that's the life I have!"

The legs of Moriarty's chair made a scarring rasp on the squeaky-clean floor tiles. He backed toward the door in the full grip of what might be a terminal spell.

"Sarah, I'm sorry, really, sorry, really. I just wanted to talk, I didn't know about Taylor's, I . . . I'm going. Bye."

He thought the engine would never catch, but it did. He avoided looking back at the door where, in other days, she would have been standing, waving him goodbye toward his day. But here the umbrella surely was folded, folded and put away.

For no reason he could name, Moriarty found himself surveying Kim's appliances. The stark white Krupps coffeemaker stood gleaming on the countertop their maid had also gleamed. Next to it sparkled the black Bosch espresso machine. Ranged farther down were the KitchenAid mixer, the Toastmaster wide-slice toaster, the Cuisinart, the under-the-counter can opener/clock/radio/TV. Then came a new model of the old Hamilton-Beech malt mixer and the wood block holding eight different French knives and the electric salad spinner. Next came the range, with the microwave oven above. The microwave was the only one of the items that got regular use. Moriarty put his beer mug in the stainless-steel double sink, on the disposal side.

In the master bedroom, he couldn't quite decide what to take. The box of things from his old home hadn't been unpacked. He could take that. And a suit, jackets, shirts, ties, underwear, socks, toiletries, a copy of his dissertation on Keats, just enough in all to fill his garment bag carry-on, although there'd be no airplane, just his old VW. He draped the garment bag over Kim's Cateye CE-3000 Ergociser. When he'd finished stuffing in the clothes, he added a small picture of Kim. In the box he had a photo of Sarah. He had none of Sandra, but he could live and leave without one. His wants satisfied, Moriarty scrawled a note to Kim.

Dear Kim,

I'm having a terrible long spell and must find shelter. Take care of yourself.

Tom

He put the note on her dressing table, next to the facial mask where she'd be sure to find it. He put his archival box under one arm and balanced the garment bag over his shoulder. He wore his London Fog zip-in-lining trench coat. An umbrella was too bulky. Riding the elevator down, Moriarty wondered about all the things he might have been or done, about all the things he might have forgotten here, at Sandra's, at Sarah's.

When the VW started, he felt relieved, almost nerveless. Out and away. Toward what didn't matter just now, although he was sure it would later. For the moment it was enough to be untriangulated, out of range. Actually, Moriarty realized, he felt so relaxed that he might just stop at the big cathedral on his way out of town and sit in the dark for a spell and think, maybe even pray, and ponder the truth of life's mysteries, like steeplechases, indeterminacy, umbrellas, and above all, trinities and kisses of peace.

# Liebestod

Peter would say today is like a *lied*. Clear and sad. The mists farthest up the mountain have lifted, uncovering the church and the house where we lived back when we were lovers. Down here wisps still cling to the tops of the lemon trees, like thin beards entangling what putrid yellow-brown fruit remains unpicked. From this window I can see Daniel's motorbike propped against the chicken-wire and olive-post fence. He's sitting at the stone table on the terrace, scratching. Behind him the stream runs to the sea through a cleft like a vulva. God, what times we had, Peter and I.

Daniel is whistling a country song. Simple progressions. Tonic, subdominant, dominant, and back to tonic. Simple and sweet, like a hymn or a lullaby. Just as banal, too, though Peter wouldn't think so. Simple and sweet, he'd buy, but not banal. Not even this tune Daniel's butchering, a ballad about babies and cowboys. Its fragments disappear in the cool foreign air. My breasts ache this morning.

I turn to the record player. That's what it is, a plain old record player. Peter and I had it with us years ago. He'd play Beethoven and Mozart and Haydn on it, sit rocking—no pun—and listen, his hand coming up every so often to conduct a passage. I, fresh out of the conservatory, said how old-fashioned and dull it was, not fresh like synthesized sounds, like tone rows, like anything I now think is mindlessly mathematical. "Nice music," was all he'd say.

"Nice music." Then he'd go off to the battered upright that the woodman had hauled from the road in his mule cart. He'd sit on the rude stool, lay hands upon the keys, and stare through the harp as though he could see the music in the strings.

His hands were small. He played tenths with agonizing difficulty, reaching beyond his grasp. I could reach them easily. "Big hands," he'd say when we were in bed. He'd take them and hold them out from him against the light, studying them like a score. I put on Schumann too late to cover the noise of Daniel's motorbike starting. It sounds like a chainsaw. They have those here now. When Peter and I lived together the men used long saws. You'd hear them in the autumn, cutting the firewood, clearing the terraces. Their songs echoed from the mountains. Then the house smelled like wood smoke. Our skins tasted of olivewood. Now it's kerosene or butane. Compounds, leaving artificial residues, what's left after love made with a too-young man.

I should do something. There are things in the garden to be picked. My concerto needs finishing. Its neat equations should be arranged. The piano needs polish. I could write letters, beg for bookings. I could comb out my hair. Above the music I can hear Daniel's bike ripping up to the cafe. Gone for coffee and cognac. I suppose Peter would say, "nice boy."

Coffee—black, with a crescent of lemon in it. I remember coffee taken in a garden in Granada. I'd finished mine quick. Those days I was in a hurry. I made notes, dashed off to see a frieze, a fountain, a place where Moors gathered to hear the muezzin. I collected objects and experiences then for what I imagined was the future. That day I found a small piece of wall carving, about the size of my metronome, discarded in a rubbish pile near where masons were restoring a wall. The figure looked like a lutist. I wanted it to mount on green velvet for our house on the hill by the church. I hid it in my waistband, pulled my blouse out over it.

I remember coming back for Peter. I found him sitting on a bench, his head cocked to one side, faintly nodding. His legs were crossed. One hand held his cup. The other conducted music. I heard only birds and insects, the whine of tires on asphalt, the thump of a diesel truck. "Nice sounds," he finally said, and then, "you look pregnant." He carried my lutist out in one hand. The other still conducted.

One morning a while later, after we made love, he sat at the old upright and began to compose. My project was decorating. Nesting, I guess. I'd hung the carving over our bed as soon as we got back. He started with an engine noise, a repeated bass note played against the sound of his right-hand fingernails scraping the wood beneath the keyboard. Then bird noise rose as he rubbed, plucked, tapped the strings. His voice made shrill sounds, like katydids rubbing their legs. Every morning for weeks, he worked on it. Toward the end, I thought I was pregnant, but I wasn't.

I heard that piece performed not long ago, on the BBC World Service. The engine, and then the birds, the bugs, fruit plopping on the mosaic walks, water plashing, a high call to prayer, shuffling feet, the cries and hammers of the stonemasons, all of it swirled into the finale, a great birthing crescendo. Years ago that we were in the garden.

I can't work today. Daniel will be back soon. He'll want to

eat, take a walk, and then make love. We'll end the day getting drunk in the smokey cafe, pelted by racket from the video game, from the TV. Tomorrow morning I'll sit here again staring at these blacks and whites.

Peter's dying, I heard.

Her letter came, borne by Castor the postman, whistling his way through the mist to my door. She's German, sad as Schumann, heavy as Wagner. Or at least so Peter said. He thought I was Celtic, mostly improvised. A tune for pipes, whistles, fiddles. The sentimental fool.

Dying, the letter said.

Full of growths. She thought I should know. And he'd decided not to take the therapy, the chemicals and deadly rays. He would fast, try to starve the cancer out. I knew why. He wanted to finish his last work. His symphony. Something their small son could remember him by.

Outside the mists are all gone, blown away. I watch one rotten lemon fall from a gnarled tree. These keys feel cold and dead. I'd like to be seized, just once. Force something out for him, something sad and clear. I'd play it for him with my big hands. Play it again and again until he mounted into this bright air. He'd be nearly transparent from his hunger, and I could see the sun through him. We'd be light as gracenotes, joyous as echoes. "Beautiful," he would say.

Impossible, of course. The motorbike will whine back soon. Life's jingles will carry us along. I finger the cold keys. The harp is quiet. I hear only my heart's slow rhythm.

# A Post-Modern Instance

I saw Gerald's and Susan's changes, but like one observing a glacier it was hard for me to know just how, and how fast, they came. His progress was plainer, I suppose. Big, glib, alcohol-flushed, he strode, and sometimes ran and sometimes crawled, through their marriage as if it were an emotional jungle gym ready for the wild swing out with legs extended, palms burning against the hand-worn chin bar, chest full like a mountain gorilla's of a cry that was both triumph and despair. She, naturally, noticed the cry, because she was full of her own, many of them unvoiced. Largish, auburn-haired, with a quick, quixotic humor that took more than it gave, she stood for their vows in the way she understood them, as laws, much as if saying "I do" had installed traffic signals, red and green and caution, into the brain.

Gerald never acknowledged signals, though. That I learned early on. He'd come home from work full of his day, and full of beer, and full of dreams: "Let's go to Morocco, to Mongolia, to Nauru, to Nebraska, we'll live in tents, yurts, grass houses, soddies, we'll live off the land, off welfare, off inheritances, off beat." All the time Susan was signaling that dinner was ready, that she had ideas, too, that she wanted a kiss. Meanwhile, I was semaphoring that I existed somewhere down around knee level.

I will say this. After an obscure uncle left him some money, Gerald did take us a lot of strange places. I won't soon forget the walk from the higher lands down to Katmandu, clutching Susan's hand to avoid getting lost in the crowd of Tibetans fleeing the Chinese invasion. Three days we walked, out of money and with only some bread and cheese, before we spotted Gerald coming toward us in a Nepalese Police Land Rover. "Thank God you're safe," he shouted again and again, explaining again and again that he'd had to fly out and leave us in order to come back for us, and there had been only one place on the mail plane.

"What happened to women and children first?" Susan had asked.

"This was man's work," Gerald replied. And then we were off to watch some Buddhists whack the head off a buffalo in a blood rite, with Gerald recording the chants and cries and Susan covering my eyes. There were other dream-fulfilled places, too. Molokai to lounge in native splendor for a month or so. Beijing on a business trip, but that was all gray and polite. Mexico to explore the Mayan ruins and record the mushroom rites. Gerald and Susan both took the mushrooms. Gerald got sick and saw only monsters, he said, with the heads of his various bosses, each with ferocious teeth that tore him to shreds in vivid Technicolor. "Just like real life," he said. "What kind of hallucination is that?"

"You weren't in a state of grace," Susan said.

"So, what did you see?" he asked.

And I remember what she said, with the *bruja* and me watching, as we had for the four hours of their staring and dancing and thrashing. "I saw a perfect oval," she said, "and it glowed like the egg of creation, from within, gold and blue and pink, pulsating like a heart, and then it opened, not like an egg breaking but as if it had divided like a cell, and out came a white vapor tinged with amber, and then through that came figures, hundreds, thousands, of figures, or really just coloring-book outlines of figures, animals and people, birds and insects, all in the vapor, and then I heard and felt a great wind and the vapor and figures blew away, seeds in the wind, and there was nothing except a blue field, like a perfect summer sky, and then the sky started to darken, not becoming cloudy, just darkening, black being added to the blue, and I saw two figures coming out of the sky, a man and a woman, naked and anatomically correct, but without faces and they were light against the dark, coming toward me, getting bigger and bigger, until they were right there"—and Susan held her arms straight out—"and I was frightened suddenly, and cold, and then I saw their faces, and they were my parents, and then yours, Gerald, and then they became you and me, and then as though someone had poured acid on them they started to dissolve, to drip and run, candles in the sun, until they were just puddles at my feet, and I heard music, either a dirge or the wedding march. Everything started to whirl then, like a pinwheel and, after that, I just saw colors, and I started to come down." Susan stopped then, while the *bruja* sat like a Mayan sculpture and I held my knees in amazement and anxiety.

"So, you had a good trip," Gerald had said over his cup of mescal. "But what did all that mean, anyway?"

"I don't know," she'd said. "Let's go buy some pottery."

Not long after that, the trips stopped. The uncle's money only went so far. Besides, Gerald seemed to have decided that, if he wasn't in a state of grace, the hell with it. "Let's stay home, make some money, party hardy."

By then I was so occupied with adolescence and school that I really didn't want to go anywhere, not with Gerald and Susan anyway. In fact, I wanted to stay away from them, because the changes had started, but also because I wanted to do simple things like drink too much beer myself, and get laid. I did. The first was better, at least until I practiced the second. That was what Gerald was doing, too, I learned in the easy, clichéd way, one night in a saloon far from home. There he sat, in mountain-gorilla form, chest puffed out and paws draped around, I admit it, a stunning brunette, oblivious to me trying to talk the bartender out of a six-pack. It wasn't till I got to the car, carrying the sack by the neck, that I felt anything, and then it was like seeing him in that Land Rover in Nepal: astonishment, followed by a slow hurting, like you'd twisted your ankle on something you couldn't see. My date asked me if anything was wrong, and I said, I think I said, with proper secondary-school cynicism, "Nothing that a Buddhist rite wouldn't cure."

Susan's red light flashed on soon afterwards, although Gerald, typically, didn't know he was sending out bad signals. Unfortunately, perhaps, I was home in the jungle gym. Gerald's appearance came as a telegram from the old days. Slamming through the door, he shouted, "We're going to the Fertile Crescent!" He exhaled alcohol like buses exhale diesel fumes.

"Why? You want another child?" Susan asked.

"No. I'm fed up. I want excitement. Travel! Adventure! Romance!"

"Romance?" Susan asked. "Romance?"

Red light. Susan pounced. Looking back, it seems to me that her back arched, and her feet barely touched the floor as she went to Gerald, who stood watching her as one might observe Fate coming on little cat feet.

But what really happened, I suppose, is that Susan faced Gerald and, with her red fingernail, touched that old talisman—the lipstick on the collar. Red to red, and the change began. To this day I cannot recall the many scenes of ordinary life, gray muslin, that must have been stitched between the bright, garish quilt pieces of these lives. The glacial slide of those scenes.

I remember a few months after the lipstick, and the shouting, after the weeks of Gerald's hypercourtesy, and the occasional love-moanings from their bedroom below where I studied for the college boards, Gerald's late boozy arrival, the gorilla's bellow, and the feline response. When I got there Susan had clawed his face and torn his coat, and now she drove Gerald toward the back door and down the steps, she shrieking "bastard, I hate you," and he flailing back bellowing, "bitch, frigid bitch," and I trying to get between them, being there but not there in some icy isolation of the spirit, and then Gerald's hand hitting home, the sound of palm on cheek, and Susan's wail, and then the deep sobs as Gerald drove away, his radio antenna bent at right angles by Susan's last, despairing act. I remember Susan holding onto me and sobbing, while I wondered what next, and what would the neighbors think, and if I would pass the entrance exams, and when I could get away from this, and Susan saying, at last, rubbing her puffy cheek, "Oh, God, you're one, too, you're another man."

I remember Gerald and a bar friend coming for his things, Susan purposefully at an Al Anon meeting and, when they finished loading the two cars, Gerald hugging me, tears on his face. "I love you, I do, you must believe that," he said, and I said I believed it. And he said, "We'll go to Kenya to see the animals and to Honiara in the Solomons for the carvings, you'll see, we'll be close." He kissed me, the Dutch courage wet on his lips, and they drove away, Gerald waving until he turned the corner.

After that, a long gray stretch. Susan sat for hours, eyes in the thousand-yard stare, until the papers were served and the settlement made. She ferried me to college and wept when I finally pulled from her hug and went into the dorm, my new world. I was glad to be in it and out of theirs. Yet no one can ever leave another's world, something I didn't learn at college. No matter how hard I tried—and how I tried! with summer jobs in far-off states, and a year abroad for French study—Gerald and Susan found their way to me.

Glacial scenes.

Gerald brings his new wife to meet me. He is sober and formal. She's small, dark, as far from Susan as Nepal is from Mexico.

"Jamie," he says, "this is Nancy. Nancy, Jamie."

"I'm happy to meet you," Nancy says, and in her eyes and the grip of her hand I feel a great quiet, or perhaps a somnolence, and I wonder if such a narcotic is what Gerald's needed. We go to a good college-town restaurant and eat good steaks and drink good wine. Gerald sits holding her hand while Nancy tells me about her career as an interior designer. I chatter how I'm going to the Sorbonne when I graduate and travel a lot because, of course, that was how I was brought up, all those trips, the adventure, the romance.

"I'm much more a stay-at-home," Nancy says, "and I have the business."

When she goes to the restroom, Gerald gulps a glass of wine.

"It's better now," he says. "Really. Much more stable. It's your turn. Do it. Go for the excitement. I've had mine. Go for it." He has more wine, then looks at me with the gorilla glint.

"You remember Mexico? The mushrooms? Well, I lied. I had visions, too. I saw Paradise. It looked like an island, like in the Arthurian legends, like Avalon, all gold and blue, the Virgin's colors, and I was in a curragh, paddling like mad for the shore, but the island kept getting farther and farther away, and then a lady appeared, a fair lady, waving to me, and then it all vanished and I was in a black fog, or black water, and I couldn't see or breathe, that's when all the fanged heads appeared, and just as they were about to get me the black went away, and the woman reappeared and she pulled me to her breasts. I was safe, and felt colors and saw music. Really. That's the truth."

Gerald stops. He sees Nancy coming back. But, before she sits down, he puts his big paw on my hand and says, "God, I loved Susan. I did, I do." I wonder why he lied. When.

Glacial scenes.

I'm at Susan's, the summer after graduating, after the ceremony neither Gerald nor Susan attend, for fear of seeing one another. They send cards and money. Anyway, I'm home for a few weeks getting ready to go to Paris. Susan's anxious, so we shop for things I'll need. It makes her happy, needed. I fix meals to be ready when she comes home from work. Gerald's maintenance doesn't go nearly far enough, she says, not with inflation, and he's so unreliable, so Irish, and besides she likes the job, likes being at least semi-independent. I know all this from her letters, just as I know the family news, about her daffy sisters, and her mother, my grandmother, who's mean but very sick and rich, and so everyone's exceptionally nice to her now. I listen, though. There's a certain calm in hearing things you know. We reminisce about the trips.

"Remember the buffalo? The *bruja*? The Great Hall of the People?"

"Vividly," I say.

"Some good times," she says. When we remember she talks about Gerald as if he were a tour guide we once had.

One night I come home after saying goodbye to some old high-school friends. Not late, about eleven. Old high-school friends are dull.

"Jamie," Susan says, pointing to a salesman type slouched on the sofa, "this is Frank."

"Hello," I manage.

"Fine-looking boy, Susan," says Frank. "Fine-looking boy."

"Well, good night," I say, and again there's that slow hurting that comes not from Frank's bulbous face, or the highball glasses, or even from Susan, with her tight smile and eyes that say she'll explain, but from something cracked inside, some vessel that's oozing. A drain somewhere. Upstairs, trying to read, then trying to sleep, I hear them talk and laugh, and then go to Gerald and Susan's bedroom. When the creaking and sighing start, I put on my Walkman, listen to Debussy and Ravel until I glide off to sleep. I dream about *le mer* until the sound of a car starting in the driveway awakens me.

In the morning, over the eggs I poach, Susan explains. "I know it hurts you," she says, "but I was never frigid. Never. Now I have one-nighters when I need them. No, I was never frigid, but I did hold back sometimes because Gerald never picked up on my needs, my wants, and so I didn't want him to have *everything*. Have you any idea what I mean?"

"I think so," I say.

"Don't worry. I'll never marry again. Gerald was enough. He cured me."

"Yes, I see."

She, too, then patted my hand. I thought: how many different kinds of touches there are. I saw the corners of her eyes fill.

"We had some good years, Jamie. I suppose I still love him. In some ways. Do you think so?"

"I don't know," I say. I don't, and I'm glad my flight is only thirty-six hours away.

In Paris, there were only the letters. Exhortatory notes from Gerald, urging me to great things, great adventures, some so exuberant that the booze sang in them like sap in a tree. Newsy missives from Susan, full of family doings, her mother's alternating recoveries and sinking spells, and about the courses she was taking in archeology.

Gerald mentioned Nancy at first, but then she disappeared from his dispatches. Susan never wrote about her need-fillers. I wrote carefully passionless replies, describing the wonders of living in Paris and speaking French, of the fine courses and professors I had. Eventually I wrote of my French girlfriend, but I didn't say we were living together, or that I spent more time in cafes, bistros, and bed than I did in lecture halls. Still, my studies interested me, and I supposed that one day I would return to the U.S. to teach French language and literature. Would I be, though, a roué, a rogue professor, a Gerald's gene, or merely an eccentric, slightly naughty family person, following Susan's unbroken chromosomes? It wasn't a question I debated at length.

In 1985, I'd been in Paris nearly a year when, within a month, two startling letters arrived. The first came, predictably, from Gerald. After the usual admonitions and advice—"Singapore! There's a fortune to be made in Singapore, or at least an adventure to be had!"—he announced that he'd divorced Nancy, receiving a decent no-fault settlement, cashed in his various pensions, and was about to sail the Pacific in a chartered yacht. Would I like to crew for him? A matter of only a few months, and he'd pay my way to San Diego. Would I let him know at once? He signed off with: "I know I've done many bad, or stupid, things in my life. But I've never been dull. I have always loved you, and your mother for having you. Crossing the Pacific with my son would be the greatest adventure of my life. With all love, Gerald."

I considered his proposal seriously. But after thinking about the Sorbonne, and after Michelle's weepy protest, I cabled Gerald at the San Diego Yacht Club saying with affectionate gratitude that I simply couldn't take the time, but that I'd consider Singapore, and perhaps, if he'd let me know where he fetched up, I'd come to see him. Such a reply was the least I could do, I thought.

Susan's letter, arriving *Express,* also announced adventure and the death of my grandmother. It happened quite suddenly, Susan wrote, and grandma's profound wish was to be cremated at once, with only the smallest ceremony. There simply wasn't time for me to get there, and not to worry. Susan described the substantial money that had come to her and her three sisters and said as soon as her new will was completed, she was off to Mexico to visit ruins and maybe take the mushrooms again. Would I like to join her? "You know," she wrote, "the only thing I think I've learned so far is that life will go on, no matter what. Even the pyramids crack and give way to the stubborn grass eventually. Now I'll live my life just as stubbornly, just as I lived Gerald's, and yours, for so long." She would be leaving, probably, in a few weeks, so I should let her know if I could join her, at her expense, of course, if only in Mexico City for a holiday. That adventure seemed more feasible, and this time ignoring Michelle's Gallic suffering, I wrote that I would meet her there when she chose. I also told Susan of Gerald's sailing scheme. Again, it was the least I could do.

She replied promptly, telling me to join her at the Hotel Esplendido anytime during the third week of September, adding: "Gerald seems to be reading us better than before, don't you think? To want you with him? And he'd actually told me of his voyage before you. Imagine!" I tried imagining two discrete circles, once one, becoming congruent.

And I did go to Mexico City, but it was to arrange for Susan's remains to be returned to the U.S. The Hotel Esplendido came down on her when the killer 'quake hit. She, or what they thought was she, almost made it out, but the mammoth lintel of the entrance caught her across the shoulders. I learned she had gone again to Oaxaca, with some archeologist friends she'd made at the University of New Mexico. They'd been out dining a few blocks away when the Esplendido fell. Like all earthquakes, this one was capriciously devastating. Her friends said she'd had good visions again, strange ones, they said, all about eggs and water, like the Pelasgian creation myths. She'd been so anxious to see me, they said, she'd hardly leave the hotel. I thanked them for the information and, when the transportation details were complete, I walked through rubble-filled streets to the undamaged cathedral and prayed that she'd died in a state of grace.

We put Susan next to her mother in the family plot. I got Gerald's proposed course from the San Diego Yacht Club, and we tried to signal him by radiotelephone and satellite radio. But there was no response. He'd reached Hawaii safely, we discovered, and with the couple he'd recruited as crew, set off for the Solomons. We alerted the Coast Guard, who alerted all maritime authorities. Three weeks after I returned to Paris, Gerald and his sloop, the *Guinevere,* were declared overdue. Four weeks after that, an Australian freighter found the couple in the sloop's dinghy, bobbing in the Coral Sea 120 knots due south of Honiara. A typhoon had dismasted *Guinevere* northeast of the New Hebrides, and she'd started to break up. Gerald, they said, pushed them into the tiny dinghy, saying only two could survive in it. Through the driving rain and whirling wind they saw Gerald take to the rubber raft. Their last view was of him sliding it off the *Guinevere's* foredeck. Then he vanished in the spume, the sloop following. They thought he was a hero.

That was the last I heard of Gerald. He may be lost, or he may be out there, making for Singapore. Life goes on. I finished my degree, and married, then quickly divorced Michelle who, when she'd learned of the inheritance from Susan, claimed she was pregnant. When time disproved that, like just "another man," I went to the lawyers.

Now I teach at a fancy, mainly female school in the

Northeast U.S. Sometimes, when lecturing about the fiction that is reality, I tell about Gerald and Susan. I know, of course, sentiment being what it is, that the tale could drive five or ten students to my bed, but I detest pity fucks. No, I tell it to illustrate fouled karma. As I insist to my colleagues, who want to construe almost everything symbolically, if Gerald's and Susan's lives meant anything beyond themselves, it is simply that they are emblems, icons, of some modern lives.

Even so, often enough at night, I get strange signals. I dream of a man in a curragh paddling toward a woman on an egg-shaped island. From wherever it is I am, I urge him on, I implore her to reach for him, to hold him to her. But he never quite makes the shore. He disappears into blue water with dolphins playing around him, and she vanishes in the blue and amber vapor of her egg. I dream this often and, when I awaken, I turn to the photo on my bedside table, a picture of Gerald and Susan and me as a boy, and then I mourn them, miss them, as only an only son can.

# The Fickleman Suite

## Praying for a Fickleman

Henry Fickleman knew the truly bad stuff had started coming down when he found out his lover's husband was praying for him. On his knees, hour after hour, like Francis of Assissi repeating the Jesus Prayer. Except the prayer Henry Fickleman's lover's husband prayed wasn't religious, or even vaguely theological. Henry's lover's husband learned it at the New Era Consciousness clinic where he'd gone after nearly drinking himself to death because he discovered Henry was having his wife. The prayer went:

> Great Transactor, please keep me hating the man
> who made me alcoholic. And while you're at it, lay
> a load of shit on him.

Henry Fickleman knew the prayer because just after they'd finished, his lover recited it for him. Henry was untying the last rope, when Thelma chirruped, "Barney is praying for you. New Era said it would help." Thelma rubbed her wrist and took a swig of wine while Henry pondered this.

"How will it help him?"

"I don't know. He said the theory was that hating somebody makes you feel better about yourself. You'd be OK."

Henry thought more about this. Not just about this, because Henry couldn't ever think about just one thing at a time. Also flitting through his belfry were the usual nagging apprehensions: his wife would catch them here doing genteel bondage in the little attic hideaway he'd rented when passion had become imperative and it had gotten too cold to screw in his Winnebago; his daughter's braces were too expensive; his son's soccer game was tomorrow; his bank overdrafts were killing him. Then he thought about how Thelma fornicated like an especially depraved Roman noblewoman. That brought him back to Barney's praying.

"What exactly does he pray?"

Then Thelma had told him. Henry admired her breasts while she spoke.

"Why is he praying for a load of shit to fall on me?" Henry finally asked.

"I think he wants something bad to happen to you."

Henry thought again how perceptive she'd become since he'd rescued her from housewifely boredom. Before their affair she'd been a club-belonger and coupon-clipper and cheerer at her kids' athletic events. Now she was a *Woman With A Past*. Her husband was a *Reformed Drunk*. And Henry, it seemed, was a *Target*.

"Has he said he'd do anything?" Henry asked. He took a swig of Miller's from a quart. "Like, would he tell Helen?"

Helen was Henry's wife. She was everything Thelma had been but, so far as Henry knew, she had *No Past*.

"He wouldn't do that." Thelma said. "That would mean he's not OK."

"Would he tell my boss?" Henry wasn't exactly afraid of his boss, but he was cautious. Times were hard, and there was no shortage of people to peddle RVs. As for being hurt, Henry had a large, subterranean fear of pain. He hadn't been to the dentist for three years, even though he could feel little holes with the tip of his tongue and his breath was sometimes difficult to manage.

"No. They taught him at New Era that it was *his* problem. He's got to get OK. Besides, I hid his gun."

Thelma liked to sit and talk after sex. Henry liked to go home, so they were sitting and talking. Henry pondered Barney while Thelma switched on *Hill Street Blues* and said how she hoped Frank and Joyce would stay together. Henry remembered when Barney had found out. It made him wince and drink more Miller's. Thelma opened a can of peanuts.

They'd been in bed, in Barney and Thelma's big king-sized water bed, back when the affair was fresh. He'd met her at the Outdoors Show. She was taking fly-fishing lessons, he recalled. Tossing a tiny plug into a floating yellow ring. He'd made a lewd remark about the sexual significance. She'd laughed. Later, they'd gone for drinks. There followed lunches, dinners, drinks—a three-week seduction game until she'd at last, one halcyon spring day, made the Winnebago sway like a cattail in a tornado. Ever since, they'd been a number, so familiar in dark bars that waitresses didn't bother to ask what they wanted, just stumbled over with a bourbon Presbyterian and a Miller's. A year into their relationship Barney stumbled in, too. They shouldn't even have been at Thelma's, of course. But the Winnebago was in the shop, and Thelma swore Barney was safely off on his rounds as a produce man, schlepping artichokes, pomegranates, kiwis, and damsons. There they'd been, frolicking like seals atop the big water bed. Then they'd heard the front door open.

Thelma behaved well. Lace under pressure, Henry called it. She bolted from bed, struggled into her filmy undies, and charged toward the top of the staircase.

"Darling, you're home," she shouted at the startled Barney, who, in a spasm of uncertainty—was he whom she meant by "darling"?—dropped his clipboard and Budweiser and rushed the stairs. In a way, he was lucky, Henry supposed. He did have on shorts and T-shirt when Barney stormed into the bedroom, arms wrapped tightly around the lissome Thelma who was backpedaling like a cornerback.

Barney's look still haunted Henry. Not exactly that of the bludgeoned steer, but close. The look one might have on opening the refrigerator and seeing a little man at the light switch.

"Argggggghhhhh!!!!!" was how Henry recollected Barney's greeting.

"Mr. Malafort . . ."

"Barney," came from Thelma, standing prim as a Maidenform matron between them.

"Arrgggghhhhh!!!!!"

Then Barney Malafort had run, taking the stairs down three at a time. Henry and Thelma heard the door to the liquor cabinet open and slam shut. They heard Barney's feet kick his clipboard, and the clipboard's skitter. They heard the front door slam and the car go away. Then Thelma had wanted to talk. Henry had wanted to go home and hide, or drop in on TWA for a Getaway to Samoa. In the end both had their way, except for Samoa. Barney Malafort had his way, too. He began serious drinking, like an Indian trying to put white distillers out of business. That night Thelma had a taste of the new Malafort. The next morning about 10:00 A.M. she called Henry out of a big RV close to tell him about it on the telephone. Barney had come in at around 2:00 A.M. Thelma heard him negotiate the stairs on all-fours. She'd watched him crawl across the yellow-green shag to the bed, pull himself up and, screaming "ARRRRGGGGHHHHH," plunge a Bic ballpoint pen toward her chest. Thelma ran for the kids' room where she locked herself in. But the pen penetrated. When Thelma and the kids at last deduced the cause of the strange gurgles and gushes, they emerged to find Barney floating peacefully in the bed frame on the punctured water bag. His tie was askew, but otherwise he was unmussed. The room resembled a rice paddy. From then on, Henry knew too well, it had been the heartbreak of dipsomania for Barney. Until New Era and this praying.

Thelma pushed the peanut can at Henry. Their aroma lifted him back to the carnal now, and he crunched a bunch between strong, holey molars. Diaphanous red skins flecked his shirt with what looked like blood specks.

"Peanut for your thoughts?" Thelma's hips, Henry noticed, had a certain thrust.

"Not now," Henry said. "I've got to think this out."

Thelma said, "Don't worry. He's sober and praying. What harm can come from that?"

On the way home to Helen's macaroni and cheese, he could not forget Barney's praying. When he saw the Grace Cathedral's neon sign—Bible Teaching, Bible Preaching, God Impeaching All Your Wrongs—Henry shuddered. Yet he knew he was no worse than most, better than some. Besides, in the modern world, weren't all bets off? Hell, *he* was OK. Henry arrived at his safe split-level in a cheerful mood. He enjoyed the macaroni and cheese, admired his daughter's new braces, chuckled sympathetically over his son's new thigh bruise, and about 1:30 in the morning made love to Helen who, when it was so quickly over, rolled away from him and snorted, "You need vitamins." Henry wasn't fazed. Two women in twenty-four hours was an adolescent's dream. He had no trouble falling back to sleep, and he even squeezed in a little prayer of his own, just in case.

The next few weeks ran down their accustomed grooves. Thrice a week he met Thelma at their hideaway. In the middle of the second, they gave up genteel bondage and went to body oiling and extended orgasm practice. At a Tupperware party, Thelma had discovered that Hidden Valley salad dressing was a nice lubricant and tasted fine, too. She made Henry into a salad. Henry wallowed through their exercises like a fatted calf. One time he kept it up for forty-five minutes of rigorous rehearsal. Thelma wept with pride. Everything, in fact, was jake, until one afternoon Henry left their love nest and came upon the crudely crafted note stuck behind his windshield wiper. Manufactured of letters cut from the newspaper, it read:

> I am cured but you are Sick. I am still
> praying for you, so watch your ass.
>
> Barney M.

After that it seemed to Henry that everywhere he went he found a note. One was pinned on his suit at the dry-cleaner's. He found one on a shopping cart at his supermarket. At the RV lot, he found a note pinned to his appointment calendar saying:

> The Great Transactor is Wise. You have
> no tool to match his Prayer.
>
> Barney M.

Henry went out and had four Martinis. Barney, he thought, was going too far. Something must be done. But the office missive was as nothing compared with the next signal. This bad stuff arrived early one afternoon when he came to the love nest and found a message pinned to their pillow. Scented with gardenia and elaborate, it was composed of flowery script cut from Hallmark cards. Roses and angels adorned its handhewn deckle edges, cut, it looked to Henry, with a Buck knife. There was a cupid pasted in the middle with an arrow piercing its heart. The message scared Henry impotent.

> I have arrived at Secular Sainthood. My praying is
> increasing. You cannot escape its Force. Remember
> that and get your shit straight.
>
> Barney M.
>
> P.S. Tell Thelma I found my gun in the shoe box
> in the hall closet.

When Thelma arrived she found Henry nine inches into a bottle of Liebfraumilch. He had already been through three quarts of Miller's.

"Henry!"

Henry's filmy eyes rose to meet hers. She had seen that look before, she realized. A horrible transformation seemed to be taking place.

"Henry?"

"Thelma. He's found the gun."

Thelma started to drink, too. An hour after Henry should have left for his split-level, they were babbling, drunk, naked, and frustrated. Henry still was too worried for arousal. Thelma tried everything. Hidden Valley, bondage, fellatio, even her Little Bo Peep number in which Henry wore her panties on his head for sheep ears, and crawled around on all fours while she caned him with an old yardstick. At last they gave up.

"Thelma, what do you think he'll do? What does he mean I can't escape his praying?"

Thelma hadn't the dimmest idea. She'd never known Barney to do anything except sell produce, go to wrestling matches, and drink. Until New Era. This consciousness thing had really screwed up his pattern.

Thelma said, "I don't know. Maybe he'll keep leaving you notes, like some weird Jehovah's Witness. Maybe . . ."

"Maybe what, for Christ's sake?"

"Nothing. I'm going home."

"How can you go home to him?"

Until now, Thelma hadn't thought about it. Between Henry and her PTA and her booster's club and just normal housekeeping, she didn't have to think much. But now it occurred to her that Barney had been much easier to put up with in the weeks since he'd come home from the drying out. He no longer took drunken swings at her and the kids. He didn't throw the cat out of the bathroom window because its footfalls bothered him. Even the meetings of his support group were pleasant enough. They all just sat and talked and prayed. Occasionally they could get a little much, like when the dried-out waitress came up to Thelma and said, "Honey, you really ought to get fucked up on booze so New Era can straighten you out. It's a trip, you know what I mean." Still, on the whole, things were easier. Barney didn't even seem to care anymore about her "shopping expeditions" during which she got drunk and laid. Or else he was praying so hard he didn't notice. Really, Thelma figured, this was Henry's problem, not hers.

"Well, how can you?" Henry asked again.

"The same way you can go to Helen."

Then Thelma left, thinking how sad Henry looked trying to get his legs in his pants. She stopped at the corner 7-Eleven for coffee. By the time she got home, she felt virtuous. The kids were watching "Nova," and Barney was on his knees in the breakfast nook. With a smile she turned to a rice and broccoli casserole. About the time it was done, she later figured, Henry was signing his DWI bond at the Western Patrol Division. He'd gone through a red light on his way to the split-level and lit up the Breath-alizer at .16. Helen had come to get him. It took her four hours to get there.

"The cunt," Henry mumbled to Thelma the next day at the hideaway. He was three quarts through Miller time. "She said she really thought I should stay in jail to teach me a lesson. Holy shit, your husband is running around on a gun and a prayer, and she wants me in jail!"

"Well," Thelma offered, "jail's safe."

Right then Henry felt the bad stuff hit hard. Through the beer, and a bit of wine, he saw Thelma naked. Not just the body but the soul. She didn't care, Henry realized. Just so long as she was OK. Henry had another 32 ounces of Miller's and drove very carefully home. Coming down his street he saw a car, familiar yet strange, pull out of his driveway. Henry thought nothing about it until he found his family in the living room looking over pamphlets. His son was still on his knees.

"What's going on?" he asked.

"Well," Henry's wife said, her mouth half snarl and half rebuking smile, "I wish you had been here. This nice man, Mr. Malafort, was here. He's from, what is it, New Era Consciousness. They help alcoholics, and he saw that you'd been arrested for drunken driving. So he came to visit us. Isn't that nice?"

"What the fuck are you doing on your knees?" Henry screamed at his son.

The boy's eyes flew open like window shades, revealing pure guilelessness.

"We were praying for you, Daddy. To the Great Transactor."

"So you wouldn't get drunk and shout at us," his daughter said.

"ARRRRGGGGGHHHHH," Henry shrieked and pelted for the door.

"Wait, Henry, wait," Helen called after him. "You're

supposed to call your boss." But Henry didn't stop, and he didn't call his boss until well into the next morning. Bouncing off the handset of the 7-Eleven pay phone, his mouth was foul and fumey from the beer and whiskey he had at the hideaway. He listened to his boss toss bad stuff.

"Henry," his boss said, "I'm sorry. I didn't know. But, like Mr. Malafort says, it's always the friends of the alcoholic who're the last to know. Now, I'm a Christian man, and you can have your job back just as soon as you're well again. You just do what you have to do." Henry could hear his boss's cigar roll from one side of his mouth to the other. "I'm putting your check in the mail, Henry. Got to run now. Bye."

The phone hung heavy in Henry's hand. The 7-Eleven clerk's nose wrinkled over his pimply chin when Henry breathed on him and put sixteen little Cocktail-for-Two bottles on the counter. Mai Tais. Tequila Sunrises. Harvey Wallbangers. Piña Coladas.

"Why don't you just buy a jug?" the boy asked.

"I like variety," Henry mumbled. But he did go back for a pint of Early Times, then for another, just in case. He issued into the world burdened but anticipatory, and the walk back went well. Only two encounters: one with an uppity sweet-gum tree, the other with a small but aggressive dog. Henry counted himself lucky. Not even the note ten-penny nailed to the door of the shabby white frame house that held his and Thelma's hideaway could depress his spirits. He peered at the message. Barney, of course. But this one was personal, painstakingly lettered like a junior-high diary in Bic blue. The first lines read:

> The Time Has Come. Pray to the GT and Hold
> Onto Your Asses. . . .

Henry ripped the note in pieces without reading further. He climbed the staircase thinking about his destiny. Just now, he decided, he was OK. Very OK, careening through the stages of drunkenness.

Certainly he felt OK after the vodka gimlet, and even OKer when the dry martini oiled down his throat. Yessir, he was soon rocketing through his Jocose stage, and, booted on his way by a sloe gin fizz, bypassing Morose at which he got angry, thus paving the path for Bellicose. Henry was hell-bent for Lachrymose when the cheap door swung inward to reveal Thelma, resplendent in tight purple polyvinyl pants. She was, Henry hoped, working her slow way toward leather. Her pink polyester blouse made her breasts look like cones of bubble-gum ice cream. Henry drooled belligerently.

"Oh, God, Henry," was her greeting.

"Bullshit," Henry rejoined, with a tear in his eye. He felt himself pinballing from Bellicose to Lachrymose, having a hard time sticking in either. He was also having a hard time holding down the mess in his stomach. He felt gin molecules conducting atomic war on vodka, while rum, brandy, grena-dine, and BHA/BHT added as a preservative crawled in battle order toward his cranium.

"Oh, Henry," Thelma said again.

"Have a drink, Thelma," Henry mewled. "You can't walk on no legs. And I've left Helen, by God!"

Thelma considered her options. She could depart at once and have an early trip to the Safeway, then a telephone talk with her mother, followed by cookies and milk with her kids. Sobriety in spades. Or there was dragon-breath Henry, lips glistening and Mai Tai dyeing his teeth. Sobriety lost in one. Thelma reached for the first pint of Early Times. Henry reached for her. Six ounces later they were naked, panting, writhing on Hidden Valleyed sheets, as happy as Adam and Eve after the Fall. Henry believed he had never been happier. Oh, Great Transactor, this abandonment was ecstasy! He writhed on Thelma like a puppy on a dead squirrel. Her recip-rocating hip movements could have churned apple butter.

"Henry," she gasped once, "quit, so I can drink!" She poured Early Times into her mouth and over her chin and down between her breasts, where Henry, laughing, lapped it with great slow tongue sweeps. Lachrymose retreated pell-mell to Jocose. Bellicose was long gone. Henry was still laughing when the door swung inward, and a hairy, cold-sober hand bearing a Smith and Wesson .38 showed itself.

"I am come," screamed Barney Malafort, bounding into the attic hideaway with grizzly-bear grace. "And you're not fucking OK."

Thelma gasped, giggled, then flashed a temptress's smile.

"I don't know," she said, "I think we're doing all right."

But they weren't. Henry withered inside her. The black hole at the end of the Smith and Wesson seemed to be sucking up his soul.

"ARRRRRGGGGGHHHHH," cried Barney, waving the Smith and Wesson with as much abandon as Thelma waved her pelvis. "All right, all right, now you'll pay." He pointed the .38 at Henry's right ear. "Fuck or die," he screamed. "Fuck for the Great Transactor!" Henry gave up his soul and reached for the Early Times.

"I can't," he said to Barney. Thelma groaned and rolled from under Henry. Her hand fell on an unopened Rusty Nail Cocktail-for-Two.

An inspiration flitted through Henry's crackling brainpan.

"Here." He held the Early Times toward Barney. "Have a drink," Henry whimpered. "You'll feel better."

Barney hesitated. The moment seemed interminable to Henry, as though every cell in Barney's stone-sober brain were flashing signals through a clogged switchboard. Yet Henry counted only twenty-six seconds before the muzzle of the .38 wavered, dropped, and Barney's free hand clasped the bourbon bottle. Barney raised, tipped, and drank like a Bedouin arrived at last at his oasis. The gun thumped on the floor. The explosion didn't faze Barney, although the slug whistled into the finely cracked horse-hair plaster of the ceiling within inches of the upturned bottle. The brown fluid poured like sewage.

"Oh, shit," said Thelma, and took another pull on her Rusty Nail.

Henry smiled the smile of the truly saved. He thrust his hand into the 7-Eleven sack, drawing from it the prize of all: a Cocktail-for-Two Screwdriver. After all, he reminded himself, he'd not had breakfast.

"ARRRRRGGGGGHHHH," cried Barney. The Early Times was gone. What seemed like an orange haze wreathed his head. Barney shouted, and held out his hand. Henry deposited the second pint of Early Times therein. All three laughed, then laughed more when, after more bourbon, Barney's clothes hit the floor like dead leaves from an apple tree. "Welcome back," Thelma said. Henry retreated to the end of the bed as Barney advanced on Thelma. He perched there, screwdriver in hand, watching as Barney and Thelma heaved, then as Barney vomited and Thelma muttered incoherently. Henry looked so beatific when the police arrived, looking for the shooting victim, that they didn't handcuff him. His calm lasted through the lockup, through the hearing, even through the hangover that was a real bear.

It just plain lasted. Henry and Thelma frequently laughed about his calm, about the whole adventure, there in the mop closet at New Era, where they met every other day between group therapy and handicrafts, to make the beast standing up. They laughed, too, about their unlikely sustained passion and equally unlikely sobriety. Their new life, Henry and Thelma agreed, was not as hectic as the old drunken one, but it was OK. Besides, sobriety had other rewards. The bad stuff had lifted. Henry's cavities were filled and his breath sweetened. Their livers were healing, and they had learned to pray. They prayed daily for Helen, who had taken up with a boozey Yellow Pages solicitor. They implored mercy for Thelma's kids, who were in trouble with their school's drug counselor. They prayed especially hard for Barney, who day after day stared balefully at them from his chair across the room among the hard core. Of course, Barney still had bad stuff all over him. When he had one of his fits, Henry and Thelma had to pray even harder. It was always the same. Barney springing up and throwing his arms toward heaven, then screaming "Fuck the Great Transactor. Nothing's OK." Everyone would shake their heads as he was led away. With such an attitude, Henry and Thelma agreed, he'd never get OK again. But then, some people were weak.

# A Fickleman Jogs

Harold Fickleman took up jogging out of fear and angst. Fear of his wife, and angst over his pet amoeba that would not divide. Running, he found, loosed enough endorphins so that the two concerns blended in one great brainpan ragout. While his Nikes pounded the pavement and his lungs protested against the unnatural strain and his poor heart struggled like the sump pump in his foul basement, he saw visions of his wife as the amoeba, asexual and undemanding and single. He saw her spread out in what was both a petri dish and a sybaritic round water bed, her brunette hair like cilia, her limbs unformed, her mouth uncharacteristically shut. The vision more than compensated for the pain, and Henry found that he could call it up and embroider it the more running he did. Sometimes he'd see her smile and beckon, others she'd whisper that he was so thin and sweet and she wanted him now. Not until he stopped running would the truth re-enter his mind, like a homeowner returning after vacation: he was fat like the Pillsbury Doughboy and bad-smelling like the Michelin tire-man after too many miles, and she never wanted him, and if there ever had been a human amoeba, it was he.

"God, take a shower," Fickleman's wife would say when he came home.

"Is Daddy home?" his children would ask, staring at him sweating onto the kitchen floor.

Henry would ruffle the hair of his son and daughter to assure them of his existence, retire to scrub himself thoroughly (always avoiding the mirror) and after dressing in loose-fitting clothes, slip into the basement to check on his amoeba. That creature, at least, gave him no grief. Unfortunately, it also gave him no joy. Fickleman despaired as much of being the grand-father of a bouncing baby amoeba as of ever finding domestic bliss. He knew the call would always come from the kitchen— "Henry, supper! And wash your pudgies!"—and life would go on and on and on.

It did, naturally, until the thirteenth day of the fourth month of Henry's jogging. On that day he returned damp and breathless and endorphin-laden to his home, entered the kitchen, and received a moist, thrusting kiss from his wife.

"Darling," she cried after disentangling her tongue. "Veal tonight! Your favorite!"

"Daddy!" he heard his children call. "You're home, oh, Daddy's home!"

Fickleman knew then something destinal had occurred. He wasn't making any more money, he knew. No new car sat in the drive. No relative had died naming him as heir. The plan-ets either were in some strange conjunction, or the city had begun putting lithium in the water.

"What . . . what is it?" he stammered.

"Darling," his wife breathed, "you're thinner!" And she

kissed him again, deep and hot, before pushing him toward the shower.

That night, exhaling *cordon bleu* at each other, Fickleman and his wife made love as if Heloise and Abelard had been released from their vows for one night of passion. Afterwards, puffing like a beached whale but knowing he no longer looked quite so much like one, Fickleman made a fateful resolve.

He would become ever thinner, ever bolder, and one way or another, his amoeba would divide.

Fickleman pursued his program zealously. He ran, and ran more. He ran morning and evening. Three, five, eight, twelve, eventually fifteen miles a day. The seasons changed, and his equipage changed, but never his dedication. It paid off handsomely. His wife now could not get enough of his amorous attentions. His children now not only saw him but wanted his company. They devised phantom problems in their homework so that he could help them. They invited friends home to meet their thin, devoted father. Emboldened by his ever-increasing svelteness, by the sweeter odors of his body, he asked for and received his favorite meals, each put before him with the deference only a satisfied mate can provide. All was well. His endorphin supply was high and getting higher. The only blotch on the escutcheon of his happiness remained his amoeba. At night, after loving his wife into a deep sleep, Fickleman would go to stare at it. Wriggling there on its slide, lit through by the microscope's nova-like light, the amoeba looked so forlorn, so alone as it fitfully absorbed nutrition, that Fickleman could hardly restrain a tear. Yet he hoped.

He thought most about the amoeba's problem on his evening runs. Pounding along the sidewalks and streets, the brain chemicals beginning to churn, he wondered if somehow the amoeba was suffering what he had: fear and angst. Could that be? Of what could a single-celled creature, the simplest of God's full-formed organisms, be afraid? What anxiety could afflict it? Could it be that his amoeba, Fickleman's own, had Fickleman's former problems? That it was his mirror, like the little pug dogs that looked so like the elderly ladies who carried them to bridge games? If so, what to do? An amoeba couldn't very well take up jogging, and if it had sexual angst, as Fickleman not long ago had endured, of what variety could it be? Was part of his amoeba unwilling to separate from the rest, and if that were so, what did it mean? Humans coupled for sex. The process for amoebae was the opposite. So if an amoeba refused to divide, did that signal that it *did* have sexual dysfunction, and if so, how to cure it?

One night in late spring while running a steep hill and pondering such things, Fickleman's endorphins peaked as never before, and he thought he saw an answer. Certainly he saw something. Visions, he was back to visions. As though from a great height, he saw himself lighted by an internal sun, clear and transparent, nearly invisible, the protozoan creature. Yet he was a man, albeit quite small. He had flailing feet, straining heart and lungs, swollen nostrils, even a tiny penis shifting in its miniature athletic supporter. And he was thin, Giacomettian thin, he saw, a thin, transparent man, running. Most curiously, he detected in that image the answer to the dilemma of him and his amoeba. To achieve happiness both of them first required clarity, inner and outer, and then the Other, which consisted for both in another being. The tricky thing, Fickleman saw, was that the Other was both a piece of oneself (literally for the amoeba) and another creature (like Fickleman's wife). That's where the running came in for him, to achieve the clarity necessary to *be* oneself *for* another creature. So, he'd have to keep running. As for the amoeba, it was already clear, so all it had to do was *decide* to part itself. Fickleman's body ran on until at last, slowing, he felt himself rejoin it. He stopped and looked around.

What he saw startled him. Somehow he'd jogged into the black ghetto, miles from his home. High-rises scarred by

Magic Marker graffiti lined the street. Garbage sacks, torn by dogs, scattered remains of fast-food and food-stamp meals on the sidewalks. Music blared, echoed, from hallways and barred windows. Some kids shot baskets at a bent hoop, lighted only by the sodium-arc streetlight's orange glow. Clumps of young men stood in gesticular conversation. Fickleman looked at his blue-and-white Adidas running suit and felt afraid. Fear became fright when one clump started toward him, hydra-headed and foreign, chattering jive. Yet Fickleman could not move, could not run. They came on, high-spirited and strangely beautiful, glowing ebony and chocolate in the orange light. The voices, the figures, reached and enveloped Fickleman, and he felt his muscles tighten, his throat close. And then they were past him, moving on, neither their pace nor their conversation slowed. Fickleman peered after them, rooted in wonder, until he realized what had happened. They hadn't seen him! He had become truly, absolutely transparent.

With a soundless laugh, Fickleman started to run again. He ran through a suburban mall, through department and book and record and jeans stores, never catching the slightest sign of recognition. Neither did any odor give him away, although he felt himself sweat. He observed babies struggling to stay cocooned and teenagers fighting to become butterflies. In a fitting room he watched a woman look at herself with disgust, heard her curse her flesh as he had once cursed his. In a sporting goods store he felt a man's temptation to a gun. He saw fear and angst in a quadrille of consumption. He ran on, through a cemetery where vandals cavorted as if the dead cared that monuments were defaced. He sat in a diner with nighthawks settled in to nurse a cup of coffee for hours. He padded through the posh residential areas where the wealth was palpable in the lawns and the guilt in the alarm systems. Fickleman, fleet and tireless as Mercury, stood in front of hookers whose puffy eyes stared through him into the night. He slapped along lanes where lovers rehearsed lies of passion.

He leaned through cruiser windows to see cops cooped. He peeped into parlors, kitchens, family rooms, showing himself to unseeing citizens. He flitted through nursing homes, hospital halls, airplane hangars, watching decrepitude and illness and skill—seeing all, yet unseen; touching, yet untouched. He was, he realized, a scientist of sorts, and everything, everybody could be in a petri dish, or maybe were. When dawn approached, Fickleman felt the endorphins abate. He turned for home, running toward the rising sun, lighted like his amoeba, within and without. He ran with cilia extended, but he was not afraid.

Fickleman found his wife asleep at the kitchen table, her head cradled in her folded arms. Tear streaks traced through the powder on her cheeks. He kissed them, and she stirred, opened her eyes, saw nothing, and went unconscious again. Upstairs, Fickleman ran his hand over the tousled hair of his son and daughter. They, too, moved, sat up, looked through him, and fell backwards to sleep. How odd, he thought, that before when he was corporeal to the max they did not see him, and now when he was transparently thin, they also could not perceive him. Where was the correct point of existence, the point where he was both himself and them, or where the amoeba was both itself and another? The point where fear and angst stood still? Fickleman left his sleeping family for the basement.

The light seemed to startle his amoeba. It flinched, and its dark nucleus seemed to blink. One clump of protoplasm elongated, extended a peninsula of essence, a pseudopod. The animal undulated in a dance of being. Fickleman wondered if it saw him, perhaps looking up through the lens into and past his eye, into Fickleman's own essence. Could *it* see him? Did it cerebrate? Fickleman extended his index finger toward the amoeba. Strange, how he could see himself, just as he had always been, while others could not. Had he then changed? It was the old one-hand-clapping conundrum, the hoary tree-falling-in-the forest riddle, and he could not solve it.

His thin finger approached the amoeba. Through the lens his digit was feeler-like, a transparent wand of flesh around a wiry bone. The amoeba seemed to sense its coming. The animal strained toward Fickleman's finger, wriggled out another pseudopod. Fickleman moved his finger a few millimeters. He watched it touch the extended protoplasm, saw the amoeba recoil, swirl in on itself, and start to shrivel. He jerked his finger out of the microscope's field of vision. Oh, God, he had killed his amoeba, when all he had wanted was to give it himself. Eye soldered to the scope, he watched the animal thrash as if in a death agony. And then it slowed, stabilized. It seemed to add a pinkish tint to its transparency. The nucleus darkened, thickened, and then in a slow undulation, the amoeba pushed out from itself another self. Oozing from its side came its Other, its completion. Fickleman's amoeba had divided, and in its division become one. Lord, he *had* given it love, sex, courage, and joy. A tear blurred Fickleman's vision. He bent back from the microscope and clicked off the light. His amoebae no doubt would want to be alone.

Fickleman looked down at his body. It was thin, all right, and he could not smell himself. Neither was he amoebic. He was wholly human, a man who, he realized, had literally run into himself. Now he, too, was ready to divide. And his family was ready to be the Other. Ready to touch him, and to be touched, unconditionally. Going up the stairs to his kitchen, he felt utterly fearless, without angst, and sexy. He felt himself growing more and more substantial, assuming heft and dimension and solidity. His steps echoed in the stairway. He, Henry Fickleman, had jogged into shape, and it felt very good indeed.

# A Fickleman Augers In

In the first few days after his wife left him, Henry Fickleman felt little except a faint, persistent euphoria, something that had replaced the years of death-in-life he and his wife had lived: headaches and harangues, drunkennesses and punishing sexual inattentions, physical and emotional vandalisms, contaging each with AIDS of the spirit. He clung to the euphoria like a life preserver buoying him against the returning visions of his children again at the breakfast table that morning, sleepy, chewing on toast, and chasing cornflakes around a milky bowl. The girl wore lavender feet-in PJs, the boy camouflage sweats. His wife had worn a determined yet furtive look, like a holed-up groundhog on February 2. He again saw her tilt her face up for his goodbye peck. He felt her eyelash sting his cheek.

When he'd gotten home that night, they were gone. In the tidied-up kitchen, on the table, was a note saying she had gone away to be happy, she knew he would understand, she hoped for his blessing, she would be in touch. The note ended, "Henry, no matter what, thank you." A postcard from Greece, three weeks later, thanked him again, especially for the checks he knew she would write so long as she needed his children, or him. The card, showing a jumbo jet above a paradisical island, shot Henry down from the spiral where the euphoria had borne him, diffused and fleecy as a contrail. Fickleman was left with a fist in his chest and a throbbing somewhere deep within him, a small drum dispatching a jungle telegram to his soul. After three days he made out the words: "expect nothing, look for something."

Like tinnitus, he heard this. He could not sleep. Food had no taste. At work he felt exhausted by mid-afternoon. He often cried, sometimes for a memory, a photo, an odor of perfume, flora, diesel fuel, red wine. He could not balance his checkbook. Television tormented him with portrayals of happy families. Movies drove him to homicidal musings. Fickleman resorted to long drives in the lush Missouri countryside, or short ones out to KCI to watch jets take off and land. His house became dusty and disordered, then filthy. Two months after being abandoned, Fickleman found a note from his boss on his desk. "Take some time off, Henry," it said. "You're useless to us as is." Fickleman went to his doctor. He did not tell the physician what had happened. The doctor examined him and pronounced him fit. He prescribed tranquilizers and lots of exercise.

Henry took up yardwork as his exercise. Cleaning up the sandbox he came across four rusted Tonka trucks. He sanded them to bare metal, then painted them, weeping with the spray droplets. He threw away the trucks and began drinking in the mornings, first a beer or two, then brandy and beer. He felt better for a hour or so, just as he did after masturbating.

He put in a garden: tomatoes and peppers and beans and squash. Rabbits ate the bean and squash plants. He put up a welded wire fence, then cruised the neighborhood shooting a pellet gun at his neighbors' iron lawn ornaments, particularly the bunnies. He began serious drinking at four in the afternoon. By six he could eat his frozen dinner. By nine he could sleep. He often woke to walk the empty rooms. Sometimes he'd turn out the light and cup his hand over his genitals, holding in the warmth and imagining himself as a child.

One dawn Fickleman awoke screaming, drenched in sweat. The message in his ears clangored. Trembling so that he could hardly hold a shot glass, he made a resolve By God, he *would* look for something. He called his former mistress, Thelma, with whom he once had cavorted like the king of the Sybarites, before she got religion and dried out. Still, he figured leopards couldn't change all their spots, and Thelma had possessed one of the larger G-spots God had ever created.

"Thelma? It's Henry."

"Henry who?"

"Henry Fickleman. Thelma, it's me! I'm in trouble. I need to see you. I need someone. Please."

"You need to find Jesus. That's the only way to peace, Henry. Go with God."

The telephone hung cold and dead in Henry's hand. He replaced it with a tumbler and four fingers of Four Roses. How did one *vaya con Dios*? Even after two more drinks, Fickleman had not answered this question. He studied the dustballs tumbling under the kitchen table. How sweet they were, frolicking as if innocent in the first Garden. So, he would have to find God. But how? Fickleman paced his yard, staring at his rotten vegetables, and then he saw what to do! Go to the city market and find Melchior, the black alcoholic janitor who swept the dead vegetable leaves from the sidewalks. Back when he was a normal suburban husband, Henry and family often went to the market. Melchior, he'd discovered, was an innocent savant, maybe even a prophet. He would know where to look for God and peace.

Henry found Melchior with one arm deep into a dumpster. The other held a bottle in a brown paper bag.

"What'ya after, Melchior?"

The dumpster arm flailed up with a leaky cantaloupe. The bottle arm dropped, as if on the other end of a teeter-totter.

"Breakfast, man. Whatda you think? Oh, hi, Henry. I thought it was trouble."

"Hi. Why trouble?"

"Man. Ever since Saigon fell the pressure on garbage down here has been fierce. Drink?"

Melchior's brown bag came at Henry while the cantaloupe went into a string sack hanging at Melchior's waist. Henry shook his head, partly because he thought himself above brown-bag boozing, but mostly because he didn't care for Mad Dog 20/20.

"You got time to talk?"

"Nothin' but. Let's go back of Angelo's."

Melchior swayed down the cobbled alley leading to the market square. Commercial produce companies stood on the perimeter, bins heaped with cheap fruits and vegetables they couldn't unload on the supermarkets. Two meat markets sold fatback, neck bones, chitlins, chicken wings and thighs, catfish, buffalo, and drum. In the square's center the farmers set up. Fresh produce, farm-slaughtered meats, honey, flowers, live bunnies and chicks, herbs and spices. Every day clumps of Orientals worked the bins. White suburbanites moved with forced insouciance, pinching this lettuce head, that nectarine.

"Yo, Angelo! We gonna be in back. Cool?"

Melchior patted the old Italian's shoulder. Angelo grew the best garlic in the area, forty acres of it in Big Muddy bottomland. Good years, he'd once told Henry, he made a thousand dollars an acre. Bad years, he'd go to his cousins that weren't in jail and help out by meeting a few planes coming in from Vegas.

"You can sweep some if you want," Angelo now said. "A half-pound's worth."

"Hey, man, what you think? Vampires after me?"

Melchior perched on a crate of celery. He tipped up the Mad Dog. His Adam's apple moved like a sharkfin under his wrinkled neckskin. Melchior's face came out of Ethiopia, high cheekboned, straight-nosed, thin-lipped, with startling dark eyes set deep.

"So what is it, Henry?" Melchior said.

"I've got to find God," Henry replied.

"I'm knowin' that problem," Melchior said, holding out the 20/20.

Then Henry told Melchior about his wife and children, about his job, about the drinking and the dustballs, thinking, lusting, wanting to believe. When he was finished, the Mad Dog 20/20 was gone, and Melchior's deep eyes were glazed.

"Well?" Henry asked.

Melchior rubbed his nose, then his broad forehead.

"Look to me like you don't know shit 'bout how you feel, Mr. F. What I think is you got to go lookin' for your folks and peace and all that shit, quit watchin' dustbunnies. You dig?"

"What about God, Melchior?"

The black man tented his fingers, then knitted them, then thrust them forward. The knuckles cracking seemed loud as gunshots. Oh, Lord, what was he doing, Henry wondered?

"Everywhere, man, but you *sour* here, won't see him. Look somewheres else."

"Where?"

Melchior's face opened like black papyrus.

"To find God, man, you got to *fly*. He's up *there*!"

Melchior's arm shot toward the stamped-tin ceiling, index finger extended like Michelangelo's Sistine Chapel painting.

The foyer of Butcher's High Above K.C. School stank of high-test and spilled coffee. No one sat behind the scarred wooden desk littered with manuals and charts. Above a door he guessed lead back to the hangar hung an antique wooden propeller. Henry cleared his throat. No one appeared. He peered through the grimy window at what probably was tarmac. Ah, Casablanca! But the small plane sitting there was not a fog-shrouded Dakota, just a sunbaked light aircraft, its high tail emblazoned "Butcher's." A tiny cleaver adorned the fuselage. Henry coughed again. The door opened.

He hadn't expected a woman, and certainly not one wearing dirty green overalls, and fretfully pushing auburn hair under a blue gimme cap advertising Cessna.

"Yes?" she asked, slamming a red tool box onto the desk.

"I . . . I . . . want to fly," Henry managed.

"Don't we all? You want lessons?" The woman tossed her cap onto the counter. It smelled like chamomile laced with Quaker State.

"Well, no, not exactly. I mean, I want to fly someplace." Actually, Henry realized, what he wanted badly was something intoxicating. "I mean I want somebody to fly me somewhere."

The woman's green eyes fixed on a spot somewhere near the bridge of Henry's nose. Her generous mouth arced upward in a smile that could be asking sailors for their seed or a child for a kiss. Henry smiled back.

"A charter? Let's see the man," she said, and turned for the door. Henry followed her into a large Quonset hangar, lit by hanging fluorescent fixtures and what light could pierce the grime layering the low, horizontal windows. Fifty-five-gallon drums stood here and there, sides streaked with whatever they held. Two or three red tool stands, an electronic tune-up tester, and two airplanes completed the furnishings. One plane was small, high-winged. The other was larger, two-engined, with a short snout and a hump for the cockpit. It looked like a porpoise.

"Ernie! Got a charter for you!" The green-eyed woman's voice reverberated off the corrugated tin. Two pigeons rose from a light fixture and started loop-the-looping over their heads.

A rasping sound came from the bigger plane. A door swung up over the right wing, and legs ending in workshoes appeared. Then came the rest of Ernie, a lot of Ernie. About six-foot-four, Fickleman figured, and like a tomato stake, because Ernie only scaled about one-sixty, max.

"Yo," Ernie cried and shambled toward them. Three feet away the alcohol odor was palpable as fog. At two feet, it was like inhaling an asthma atomizer

"Damn, Ernie," Green Eyes said. "You're shitface again."

"Roger and out," said Ernie. "This the charter?"

Fickleman nodded. Behind Ernie's watery, red-rimmed blue eyes, there seemed a surety, as though this pilot wasn't afraid of clouds.

"Where'd'ya want to go?" Ernie asked.

"I want to find my family and see God," Fickleman cried. "I want to *fly*!"

Ernie didn't blink. "Muriel," he said to Green Eyes, "it's test flight time. Call Edna and let's get aloft."

Ernie Butcher was a helluva pilot, Henry had to admit. Or maybe there were lots of airplane pilots around who could cram four people and two bottles of bourbon into a small plane, climb up and out of the traffic area, perform gut-wrenching aerobatics, and still never spill a drop of booze on himself. Henry himself was drenched, but he was also drunk almost as soon as they taxied to take off. He hated flight, he immediately realized, all the more when Butcher took to flying as close as possible to pigeons, crows, and any other birds he could mimic with the little Cessna. Fickleman kept one bottle screwed in his mouth, and every time the plane turned over, or looped, or dived, or did other strange movements that filled him with a dread way beyond the ordinary fear of dying, he gulped whiskey. His companions drank, too, but they all seemed to enjoy Ernie's stunts. Muriel whooped and screamed and giggled with delight, every so often throwing her arms around Ernie so that he couldn't see much. Henry's companion, the buxom bundle christened Edna, didn't whoop so much but she did like to throw herself up from the cramped seat and utter odd whimpers.

"Darlin'," she'd drawl, "this flyin' just really gets me off, you know what I'm sayin'?"

Edna was particularly ecstatic on Ernie's last great trick before they landed, when they did a dozen tight turns around a microwave relay tower stuck out in the middle of Kansas. To whiskey-sick Henry it felt like they were on a string swung by a notably nasty little boy, but Edna loved it. Her head did bongo rhythms on the cabin ceiling while she moaned "Oh, again, oh, again." Muriel shrieked like Apaches were in close pursuit. Ernie grinned like Slim Pickens riding the Bomb down, but he still never spilled a drop, not even when they landed with a few jolts. Henry didn't see him spill a drop until they were all naked in the bigger plane, and while Edna moaned, Ernie clapped him on the shoulder and said, "You'll do, Fickleman, you'll do." Henry realized that, for the first time since his wife and kids left, he hadn't a thought in the world except how in the world he would satisfy Edna and get on with the mission Melchior had in some other-worldly way led him to. In the middle of this thought, with Edna at the stick, Henry felt himself flying without benefit of this odd-shaped airplane.

The next day Henry swallowed his bile and wondered again if he was *where* or *how* he should be. Was it truly intended that he be at twelve thousand feet, horribly hung-over, headed for Miami through thunderclouds with Ernie at the controls of the strange porpoise plane and possessed of Henry's savings?

"Yessir, terrific old airplane, this one," Ernie was saying. Just then the wheel bucked and the plane dropped, sending bile and vapors up into Henry's nose.

"Terrific," Henry muttered.

"Built in England," Ernie went on. "Beagle B.206. Slow as a whale but just as steady. Carry most anything you want to carry, like that family you talk about."

"How'd you get it?" Henry asked.

"Auction. Some fool pancaked her in to southern Georgia, filled to the gills with boo, and I bought her from the DEA. Even found a little blow behind the instrument panel. Want some?"

"Blow?"

"Cocaine. You want close to God or not?"

"Not that way, and for God's sake don't you use any while you're flying." Henry's voice sounded as if he were choking on his morality.

"Hey, when Ernie flies for money, Ernie's straight. Relax, we got a ways to go. Way I figure it, we can hop from Miami to Bermuda, that's about 900 road miles, no sweat, then Bermuda to the Azores, that's 1750 miles, some sweat, then on in easy to Lisbon, Madrid, Sicily, and to wherever that place is you want, what is it?"

"Corfu. What do you mean, some sweat?"

"I mean," Ernie said, peering at the darkening day and the pelting rain, "if we don't load on extra fuel we'll end up wet somewhere west of the Azores."

"Oh, shit," Henry Fickleman said, thinking how stupid it was to have listened to a man who lived in a dumpster.

In retrospect, from the *terraza* of the Cafe Allegro in Palermo, the voyage of the Beagle could be seen as interesting,

as in the Chinese curse "May you live in interesting times."
Let's see, there had been the rainy landing at Miami, or more
properly at Fort Lauderdale's general aviation field. Had the
*chicas* merely materialized, or had Ernie used some arcane
radio code to alert them? Then, the next day, the hop to
Bermuda, with Ernie careening the Beagle as if he were bat-
tling some monstrous Triangle genie lodged in his right
frontal lobe. But they'd gotten there and somehow wound up
on bicycles pedaled by dark, fleshy native women whose white
teeth winked like plankton. Then, at dawn, they'd ascended,
bound for the Azores, two fifty-five-gallon fuel drums lashed
back in the cargo space with rubber tubing running to the gas
tanks. "If we get low," Ernie'd said, "you go back and crank
that hand pump." Henry looked at the tube duct-taped into
the main wing tank.

"Remember the spare tanks?" he now asked Ernie. "Surer
than shit," came the reply. "Hey, another beer here!"

Henry remembered. They'd sat behind the oversize windshield, staring into the sun rising larger and larger before them
into a cloudless, calm day. They'd ridden the Beagle into the
sunrise until, oh, it must have been about six hours into the
journey, a giant hand seemed to reach up from the nearly
glassy sea and pull them downward, twisting and bucking.
Henry felt now, again, the nauseating vertigo and the panic.
He saw Ernie fighting the controls, heard the strain on the
Beagle's wings, the sound of rivets fighting to pop free, the
keening of the two Rolls Royce turboprops as they struggled
for purchase on the air. The sea spiraled toward them, gently
swaying, and for a millisecond Henry, auguring in, had
thought of union with God.

Then, miraculously, they were right side up, the sea reaching for them only a few hundred feet below. The inner windshield, he remembered, was splotched with their vomit. Their
feet were wet with fuel from the drums. Henry heard Ernie
utter his only piety: "Holy crap, whatever did it, thanks." As if

in a state of grace, Ernie had then nursed the Beagle into a landing later at the Azores, arriving with ten gallons of fuel. They'd rested, then gone on through Lisbon and Madrid to Palermo. Now there was only the 450 miles to Corfu.

"What did you think when we fell?" Henry asked Ernie.

"Thought my skinny ass was grass. What'd you think?"

"I thought I was going to die, and I was scared."

"Augering in's what seein' God's all about, man," Ernie snorted.

That night Henry dreamed of a taloned sea, of harpies clutching at him, placing a thin, brown wafer on his tongue, of someone saying "Whatever happens, thank you, Henry." He felt hands on him, and he screamed himself awake to find Ernie shaking him, and himself blubbering, "I'm OK, I'm OK. What time is it?"

"Flying time, Henry. Time to drive East."

In an hour they were at eight thousand feet, flying across the boot of Italy, over the Strait of Otranto and into the azure sky above the Adriatic. The patchwork ground, Brindisi and Lecce off the left wing, the white-capped sea, everything seemed as sharp-edged and benevolent as a Wyeth painting. Inexplicably, Henry felt again the euphoria. "There she is, Henry," Ernie said, jabbing Henry with his elbow. "Looks kinda like a shillelagh, don't it?"

Fickleman peered out. Corfu did look like a club, its handle pointed southeast toward the other Ionian islands. Due east, a sliver of sea away, loomed what Lawrence Durrell had called, hadn't he? "the dark shadow of Albania." Henry's guidebook said Durrell and others thought Corfu might be the island of Ulysses, where the great traveler had at last fetched up to confront Penelope and her suitors.

"They say come on in," Ernie reported. The Beagle banked into the sun, then west, and set down with hardly a screech. They taxied to the private aviation area, past 707s and 747s bringing in tourists by the hundreds. Customs clearance was perfunctory, their passports were stamped, they changed money, and they were there at last.

"So what's it to be, Henry? What'ya gonna do?" Ernie asked in the bus headed for the old town of Corfu.

"Find them, I guess."

"Figured that. But what'ya gonna *do*?"

What Fickleman first did was simple. Henry led Ernie to a cafe after the bus deposited them in the Italianate main square. They drank four beers apiece. "Jesus God, they got ginger beer here," Ernie said. Then, following the waiter's advice, they went to a cheap hotel on the north waterfront. Red and blue Corfiote boats bobbed in the greasy bay fronting the place. Henry bought four nights' lodging for Ernie, the *drachmas* falling from his hands like play money. He handed Ernie more *drachmas* and said, "Wait for me until Friday. If I'm not back, take off, OK?"

"Friday, OK, but make it back." Ernie took Henry's hand.

"Henry?"

"Yes?"

"Good fuckin' luck."

Fickleman stood on the road in the diesel stink of the departing bus's exhaust. Far below, its houses necklaced around a small bay, lay the village where his family must be. Here on the Northeast coast, just two sea miles from Albania, in Durrell's village of Kalami. He'd immediately divined his wife wouldn't have gone south from Corfu Town. That was all sand barrens. She was a woods, sea, and mountain person. That meant either the northwest or here. Henry had tried the northwest first. Traipsing from town to town by bus, trudging from taverna to taverna, he'd asked about an American woman with two children. No, not the usual sunburned, be-cameraed tourist. A pretty American woman with a deter-mined set to her mouth, accompanied by a little boy and girl. Several suitcases. Had they seen such an entourage? Henry combed the coastal towns. He hiked to the high inland villages, through the pine and myrtle groves, along paths garlanded with wildflowers so vivid they made his teeth ache. He'd knocked on the doors of the small pastel villas that splashed colors through the silver-green foliage of the olive trees. In English, in guide-book Greek, in smatterings of Italian and Spanish he'd inquired, only to see the shaken heads, the spread hands, the shrugged shoulders. Three days' worth, through Gouvia, west to Pantocrator and Palocastrita, back northeast to Perithia and Loutses, on to the head of the cudgel, Kassiopi, where he'd looked out into the Adriatic at what the locals said was the skeleton of Ulysses' ship but was really just a series of jutting rocks. At Kassiopi he'd gotten drunk in a waterfront taverna, danced like a Greek and, in an extremis of boozy frustration reeled off the dock into the bay. Greeks fished him out and gave him the island's specialty, kumquat liqueur. It was then that one native, who had lived in Detroit for ten years, told Henry he'd heard of an American woman living down the coast at Kalami, with two small children.

Now Henry began to pick his way down through the cork trees toward the village. A road wound down to the beach, but that was slower, and it would be dark in less than an hour. He encountered several fenced terraces below the road, speckled with sheep droppings. In *Prospero's Cell* Durrell had written fondly of the sheep, but Henry Fickleman cared for none of that now, not for Durrell or Homer. The sheep and wire were just in the way. He descended another terrace to come smack upon a dark, silent villa, nearly hidden in the trees. He'd reached the edge of Kalami.

Below, the sun's late rays played on the nearly motionless sea. Albania surely did hulk in the distance. He could see other darkened villas now, too, left and right and below. In the middle distance southwards and just above the water stood what had to be Durrell's famed White House. His guide book said now it was a *pension*. It, too, was dark. But nearer, three terraces below and a few hundred yards south, a yellow villa beckoned with lights and faint domestic sounds. He heard the brookbabble of children and a woman's voice, clear and high, cutting through. The language was English. Fickleman trotted toward the villa. He straddled another fence, then kicked through the coarse stony soil toward the lights and sounds. He panted up behind the villa, above a red tile terrace flanking its southern side. A Cinzano umbrella shaded a white metal table. Beneath the table two small children played with toy cars. Seated in a chair that matched the table sat a pretty woman, dressed in American Levis and a sweater, holding a largish *ouzo*. Fickleman took in breath to speak. As he did, a door opened onto the terrace. A tall, slender Greek, his face like that on Alexandrine coins, stepped out. The man glided to the table, reached down, and ruffled the children's hair. They smiled up at him then returned to running the cars on the tiles. The man bent to the woman. Her lips came up to his. "Hi," she said. He moved his lips to her ear, sweetly and lightly. Henry moved, dislodged a stone that rattled down to the terrace. The woman's eyes clicked up toward Fickleman. They opened wide, and through them Henry saw an ember going out. Fickleman expelled his breath. In his ears echoed "Whatever happens, Henry, thank you." Then he was running pell-mell through the cork and olive trees, his feet slipping on the sheep shit, his heart somewhere up close to his jaw, his eyes filmed as if by Vaseline.

He ran along the terrace, down toward the village, as though from death, or life, itself, and then it was that he careened into the village churchyard, and his quest ended. He found God. There on the chapel wall, His hand raised in blessing, smiled a billboard Christ. Henry blinked, felt the salt sea in his eyes, then felt a great weight rise toward the lights of an outbound aircraft, contrail pure against the wine-dark sky. Right! Bless us all indeed. Joy to his Penelope so well-ensconced with her suitor! Joy to me, too, who after all had searched and survived!

Fickleman roared a laugh out over the bay toward Albania. Leaving the chapel, he sauntered toward the beach road, feeling that strange expectant euphoria once more. But *what* to expect now that he'd sought and found, now that he truly deserved thanks, no matter what? Well, for starters how about a hell of a good drinking and womanizing weekend with Ernie, and then some flying, and then, why not? a new life. *Butcher and Fickleman Explorations* had a nice ring to it. They could take people to look for all kinds of things. They could hire on Edna and Muriel and Melchior, and Thelma could come aboard, so long as she jettisoned abstinence. Why the hell not, Henry bellowed at the lowering sky, and then he stuck out his thumb for a hitch to the city.

# A Fickleman Goes South

The one conviction Harold Fickleman now possessed was that he had no convictions. DUIs and endorphin-highs and things like that notwithstanding. And so, trembling with fatigue in the echoing cavern that was the Belgrade air terminal, looking at more luggage than he could carry, Harold was not convinced, yet, that coming to this crazy quilt called Yugoslavia was a bad idea. Maybe not starting well, he told himself, but then, his journey had barely begun.

He reached deep into his trench-coat pocket, closing his fingers around an airline vodka. The medicinal taste, the sharp ethanol smell forced his jet-lagged eyes wide open. Russians, he decided, they had to be Russians, there standing patiently on queue next to Himalayan piles of luggage and string-wrapped boxes. Muscovites, Stakhanovites, Minskites, Pinskites,

Linzites, whatever they were, come to shop in this cupboard-bare socialist country that was less cupboard-bare, barely, than their own. Patient and fretful as sleddogs they stood, waiting to board some Ilyushin aircraft for a return to their Eleusinian Fields, each apparatchik laden with loot. Fickleman sighed. But who was he to say? He was here, too, laden more heavily. They were soulmates, these Russkies. And they had vodka.

Fickleman began his trek toward Russians. Over his left shoulder hung a camera case. In his left hand he gripped an overnight duffel and the handle of a heavy suitcase. In his right hand he grasped the handle of a heavier suitcase. With his right foot, then his left, he pushed his father's old sample case meter by laborious meter. Damn those books, damn them to hell, he muttered with each shove. Moving thus, imagining himself an Armenian peddler, he arrived, puffing, at the chattering minions of the old Evil Empire.

"Pardon me," Harold said, holding up his empty airline miniature Smirnoff. "Do you have any of this?" Eyes swiveled to him, mouths opened, the line swayed like a wind-blown wooden bridge. The females turned away, as if from Satan, but one bearish man peered out from crinkled, red-rimmed eyes, laughed, shouted "Da, da!" and thrust a bottle at Fickleman. With a gusto worthy of Henry, his drunken brother, Harold lunged, uncorked, lifted, and swallowed. A millisecond later, or so it seemed, the detritus of his airline meal arced toward the bear-man, and Harold felt the cool asphalt tiles of the floor massaging his cheek.

In the office of the airport *milicija*, Fickleman found himself revealing more than he had to counselor or divorce lawyer. Perhaps that was because this questioner had plenty of time, charged no fees, and possessed the power to send him to a drying-out clinic of most rigorous manner. How ironic, Harold thought, when it is my brother Henry who's the industrial-strength boozer. Or was, anyway.

"You are being tourist, no?" the man was asking Fickleman.

"Tourists are guests. Guests do not cause trouble and vomit on other guests." Under his close-cropped brown hair and above the gray collar of his tunic, the inquisitor's face sat sallow as a rotten shallot. "You go maybe to nice *bolnica* and they cure you. Then you go home and be sick on Americans. OK?" The man's eyes lay heavy, testifying that the burden of ordinary life was enough without the onerous chore of Fickleman. Far off, Harold heard flight announcements, and the whine of jet turbines.

"I want to speak with my embassy," Fickleman said. His mouth felt as if he had brushed his teeth with sewage. Specks of vomit glared from his suit coat. "Please."

"OK," the man said. "First, though, you talk to me. Why you are wanting contact with Russians." The man opened Fickleman's passport. "Mr. Pickman, tell me please. Just to drink with them? Why are you having so much luggage, and why this paper from treacherous Republic of Macedonia saying you are making talks there? You do not seem like *profesor*."

OK, OK, Harold thought. You want the story, I'll give you the story. Fickleman leaned forward to engage the weary eyes. "It began with my pet amoeba, and then it went to my jogging, and now I'm here. Do you understand?"

On the night plane to Skopje, Harold recalled with something akin to pleasure that talk with Lieutenant Pavlovski. Language barriers or no, he felt that the Lieutenant now understood something about Harold Fickleman, the man, and his problems. What better proof than that the good Lieutenant had, with eyes rolling like marbles, waved him out of the *milicija* office and onto this JAT airliner, even providing an escort to assist with the luggage. Honesty in all things, his mother had taught him, was always the best policy, except in legal matters. What better proof than that a Slav stranger, and he, a stranger German-American, should come to terms. Besides, what was not to believe?

"I *am* a *turist, da,* he'd told Lieutenant Shallot Face, "and I am an expert on amoebae." He told the stranger about how he, Harold Fickleman, had been unloved by his wife and children and his pet amoeba, until he'd taken up jogging, become thin, and solved the vexing problem of the Other: simply divide like the amoeba, touch the Other and envelop it, commit to it, make the Self and Other One. Harold told Pavlovski of running until he'd become invisible to others and so could participate in their lives, touch them, and so heal the hurt of being unloved. He related to his Slavic auditor the great reunion with his wife and children, of his joy, and then of the hurt that could not be healed when his wife left him for a forest ranger. She took the children, he cried to Pavlovski. "They all moved to Oregon, to a cabin, and now all I get is Nature Conservancy postcards at Christmas."

"Your wife? She move to other man?" Pavlovski had asked.

"Da."

"To woods? With your children?"

"Da."

"Ah, Pickman, I would set fire to woods," the Lieutenant counseled. "But why your wife go to woods? Not happy with lovemaking, or maybe too much with amoebas, not enough with she?"

Fickleman told him. Not enough anything, she'd said. Money, lovemaking, excitement. "You and your amoeba and jogging and Other are terminally dull," she'd said. So she'd taken up nature walks and, not long after, nature couplings with Walter, the forest ranger. After that there were the papers, the chill of the courtroom, the blurry good-bye to his children—"you'll be glad in the end you let me take them," she'd said—and now this, a trip to a place as far away and foreign as he could arrange.

"Pickman, I must know. Why you do this with Russians?"

"The Russians had vodka, that's all," he told Pavlovski. "I

wanted to be drunk. I wanted to *be* someone, do you see?" Pavlovski's brow furrowed, then relaxed. A small smile cracked his lips.

"I see," came the reply. "Here it's the same. Everything insanity, so we spend all moneys on drink. I see this. I want to be drunk forever, so I drink night gone. I have brother who drink day gone."

"I do, too!" Fickleman exclaimed. "My brother Henry!" It was after Harold told the story of Henry's marital problems, and his quest, that the Lieutenant's eyes had begun a slow roll. No wonder, it now seemed to Harold, sucking down a vile red wine with a name all consonants. Poor Pavlovski could hardly be blamed for marveling at such correlations. He told the Lieutenant how Brother Henry had also been deserted by wife and children and how Henry had pursued them to far-off Greece, only to find them content—nay! happy!—and so Henry went back to America and set up an air-charter service. Even now, probably, Henry and his bibulous partner, Butcher, were flying, even as Harold was. Of course, as he'd told Pavlovski, there was one major difference. Henry had always lived drunk, whether drinking or not. Harold lived sober, even if drunk. Henry's trade was selling things, anythings, from recreational vehicles to naughty underwear. Harold was a scientist, a man with advanced degrees, a man of facts, a man, however, whose employer—a low-rent pharmaceutical manufacturer specializing in pirated morning-after contraceptive pills—couldn't be happier that Harold was bound for Macedonia to give lectures on single-cell creatures. Especially since the ever-hopeful USIA paid for it all. Anyway, Pavlovski had understood, Harold was sure, even the parts about Fickleman's amoeba and about running into invisibility. Why else the elaborate send-off, the two-cheek kisses, the shrug that out-shrugged even the French.

"Da, da, Mr. Pickman, such things, who can believe such

things?" the good Lieutenant had said. "Thank Tito for this federalism disaster. You go now to vomit on Macedonians. Good. You know Macedonians?"

"Ne."

Pavlovski's brow furrows returned, Harold recalled, and he'd shaken his head like a terrier dispatching a rat.

"They are like wolves and brood much. Be careful, Pickman. They have own *milicija,* too."

A sudden swerve jolted Fickleman back to the JAT 727, which seemed to be diving toward oblivion. The sturdy Serbian stewardess was babbling into a microphone. In the accented English translation Harold learned that they were about to land at Skopje, capital of the Republic of Macedonia. JAT Airlines greatly regretted the delay of "dree whores" at Beograd. Fickleman swallowed the last of his wine. His $14.95 digital twenty-four-hour watch, a going-away gift from his boss at Uterine Labs, showed 01:38. Suddenly the cabin lights went out while the landing lights came on. Craning to see out the window, Harold could make out only cloud wisps, or fog, and then came the familiar sounds of tire thump, reversed turbines, relieved exclamations from the passengers. He'd arrived, as the flood of perspiring passengers proved, moving Fickleman down the aisle and onto a 1930s-style ramp whose bottom steps, as if in a Busby Berkeley staircase routine, lay swirled in gray-brown fog. Fickleman, clutching his carry-on gear, was borne into the damp obscurity, onto Tarmac, and then dizzied by incomprehensible language and sodium-arc lights, into the terminal.

Disoriented and again shaking with fatigue, he stood blinking at the long counter upon which the luggage would be thrown from the tractor train now laboring toward them. He wanted a drink. He wanted a bed. He wanted to be in America. Harold sighed a great, deep, self-pitying sigh,

AHHHHHHHHHH. Then came to him a salving sound: an English sentence thrown into his ear.

"Bloody awful night, eh?"

Fickleman swiveled to behold the speaker, a small round-faced man with gold-rimmed glasses and an aureole of blond hair.

"You look lost," the man said. "Terrible country. Terrible people. Terrible to be lost here." A small hand grasped Harold's right hand with a soft, clammy grip. "Maynard Bellagio-Finney," the man said. "What do you here?"

"Harold Fickleman. I'm supposed to give talks on amoebae."

"Amoebae? How droll! Oh, the luggage has arrived."

With that, the diminutive Bellagio-Finney dropped his carry-on and plunged into the crowd of shouting, lunging passengers. He took Harold with him, dragging him toward the table. Oh, God, now what, thought Harold. Now turned out to be clambering over an odorous woman toward the luggage. "Tallyho!" rang out his guide's cry, and then Fickleman was up on the platform next to Maynard wrestling bags toward the exit, which was glowing orange and fog-brown. They pushed through it in time for Maynard to elbow a burly man away from a taxi and, with a tango-like step, pile into the back seat.

"Dear friend," Fickleman's little companion chirruped, "please stow the *prtljag*, especially that cracking great book-thing of yours, and come share my conveyance. You don't know where you're going, of course, so step to it."

Fickleman did, and exhaling black smoke, the Zastava lurched away into the fog and toward the city Harold had not seen but soon smelled. The odor was part chemical, part rot, part something sweet, like chocolate or sin.

Harold awoke not *to* an odor, but *in* one. He recognized it: vomit. But not his, not this time. The offender lay below him, stretched on the floor next to the divan on which Harold had collapsed. Maynard slept as if dead, his expectoration in a congealed puddle surrounding the large ashtray on the large drum that served as a table. Three wine bottles, two erect, also perched on the drum, and two smeared tumblers, a plate with the remains of goat cheese and sweet red peppers, some vilely sweet preserve that Maynard called *slatko* and many Greek cigarette butts. Harold's head felt like a drum, too, beaten by Congo tribesmen calling a parliament. But then, not to carp. Maynard had sheltered him when there were no rooms in this metropolis' six hotels. And they had eaten . . . well, what were they? Oh, the famous kabobs, and peppers, and bottle after bottle of Kavardaka wine. That's what he smelled. Peppers and wine. The odor. He must stop the odor. Carefully, very carefully, Fickleman raised himself, stepped across his comatose friend, over his luggage, and sallied to the window. With a cheese-smeared hand he pulled back the cheesecloth drape.

Lord, the sun! He felt his pupils shrink to B-Bs. Harold pulled up mightily on the window handle, pushed outward, and as he first saw Skopje by day, he also smelled it, the odor like a boiling penny putting to flight the sick smell of the room. But the vista wasn't sickening. Maynard's flat overlooked what must be a main square, a cobbled area punctuated by flower beds, with hundreds of pedestrians coming and going. Most, he saw, were headed over an old stone bridge—could that be his guidebook's *Kameni Most* of Ottoman days?—away from the modern flats and across the Varder river, toward the old Turkish part of town. Just as in the photos in the guide book the minarets thrust upward above the onion domes of the Orthodox churches, and from this height Harold could see the narrow streets, the billowing awnings, the ochres and pinks of the *stare grad,* its dark-clothed men and bright-scarved women bustling from place to place. Harold, this for sure isn't Kansas, he told himself, and took a deep snort of the smelting-plant air, suddenly feeling quite good.

"Exotic, eh?" came Maynard's voice through tooth rot and puke funk. "But stay long enough and you'll learn to hate it, and them."

"Who?" Harold kept his face toward the window. Jesus, come and sweep out this man's vapors as you did the money changers.

"Macedonians," Maynard humphed. "Don't let the name fool you. These are not ancient Greek Macedonians, these are modern Slavs. They eat, drink, fornicate, and defraud as if pleasures were virtues. Dante has not a circle worthy of them. They have less sense of modern civilization than Cyril and Methodius, those medieval alphabet-giving monks after whom their wretched University is named."

Maynard tossed Harold's toiletries to him.

"Never mind. We'll clean up for the beasts, then get some *čorba* at the University bar. And then I'll introduce you to your fellow scientists. They make Nostradamus look like Einstein. One, though, isn't so bad."

*Čorba* turned out to be a vile, paprika-red tripe soup, and the University a series of low concrete bunkers lit by pigeon-dunged overhead glass panels. But Fickleman's fellow scientists turned out to be singular—Maynard's not-so-bad one, a female microbiologist of nucleus-smashing good looks.

"Your name is *Snezana*," Harold repeated.

"Yes. It means Snow White. And your name? What means it? You must be telling me about you."

And so Harold did, oblivious to the glaze forming over Snezana's dark eyes. Midway, Maynard left the University bar, mumbling that he could no longer watch Fickleman drool over a Disney namesake no matter how dark-haired, dark-clad, and well-rounded she might be. Harold rambled on. When at last he finished, Snezana took his hand.

"You are sad man, Professor Ficklebun. Wife departs you, children live with another husband, and all you are having is guilt and amoebas. You have no believes. Maybe it's best for you to be going like your brother . . . what is he called?"

"Henry. But he went after his family. To Greece."

Snezana inclined her curls toward Fickleman.

"Maybe things are easier in this world, Professor. We have no problems with divorcing people. I have divorced two, and I have no guilts. I have no children, too. I have only my work. And my believes."

Fickleman felt her tugging on him to rise from the table. Her small hand clasped his with surprising strength.

"Now we go eat. Then you will prepare for your talk. Then maybe afterwards we will make love. You are sad, but also nice-looking man, good eyes and torso. Is all this OK?"

Fickleman blinked, nodded, and rose.

Looking back, Harold could only think again that were it not for the day of Snezana he would not be here, in Medagorje, waiting for the Virgin Mary to appear. But what the hell, that wasn't so strange. He had proof already of miracles, starting with Snezana's Slavic sensuality. Whoever named her Snow White had been hoping for the triumph of nominalism over nature. Hers was trick fucking of nearly Byzantine complication. Or at least Harold guessed so, not having had much experience beyond his wife, whose idea of passion—with Harold, at least—encompassed three minutes of missionary diffidence succeeded by elaborate cleansing. The memory of Snezana in his arms, following his *opera bouffe* talk at the bunker university, warmed him, even in this light drizzle descending from the clouds that wreathed the mountains where Tito once eluded the Wehrmacht and became fond of living in caves. Also of female goats, or so some Macedonians suspected.

Ah, that talk. Harold remembered striding through the concrete corridor with Snezana, their heels smacking, her breasts bouncing, his heart thumping. Then they turned out of the pigeon-shit-filtered light into a cavernous place full of smoke and body odor. He recalled her fulsome introduction making Harold seem like the latest Nobel laureate, then the scattered applause, and then he was standing to face the rows of earnest Slavic faces. Well, not so earnest. Some professorial-looking gentlemen were playing chess. Some students held newspapers before their faces. And wasn't there a Frisbee hurtling to and fro? Only Maynard's round, sweaty face peered intently at him over the lip of a hip flask. Anyway, Harold seemed to have made a great success, despite a few difficulties, or so he was told at the following *fete.*

"You are knowing much about our little friends," one bearded worthy had confided, between mouthfuls of sweet red peppers and sausage.

"Thank you."

"Professor Fickleson is an authority," came from Snezana.

"I'm not a professor, just a sort of scientist," Harold had said, and his hosts nodded sagely. Never mind that what Harold opined could be found in any decent college-level textbook, or that in a fit of nerves and confusion he'd mis-named several species of the genus *Amoebae,* confusing them with those of *Endaamoeba.* Worse, when he'd come to describe his own galvanizing experiences with his pet amoeba, waxing romantically about how it at last divided, just as he'd at last— before, of course, his family's defection—come into the full-ness of being, and about how he felt himself a midwife to it and by extension to a whole *phylum* of ontological experi-ences, just when he was doing that a bell had rung and the room emptied like a ruptured cistern. Alarmed, he'd begun to shout his words, and then, fearing that a fire or nuclear holo-caust had come upon the bunkered university, he'd spun to leave the podium but lost his footing and tumbled like a bro-ken pinwheel into the first row of seats. Right into Snezana's soft bosom, fortunately. "Hour is over," she'd said. "We can go now to party."

So they had, and party they did, until with much Slavic

hospitality, mainly of the lying sort ("Doktor," another worthy whispered, "your talking makes me want amoeba of my own") the party climaxed. Cheered on by Maynard, they'd thrown their glasses into their host's fireplace and launched a lurching circle dance that Harold in his intoxicated frenzy had supposed was indigenous only to Greece. Had not his brother, Henry, said so? Anyway, as they'd danced Snezana's hand felt warm, moist, and not much later, after Maynard's drunken farewell embrace and leering wink, when they were making the beast in her cramped flat, she felt about 32 degrees Celsius and moist as the Adriatic. But then came the peculiar request that brought him here, now, to Medagorje, and this rain, and standing with the pilgrims.

"Darling," she'd breathed. "Please go to this place and meet someone. I have your *karta*. You see how it goes with foreign talks? Macedonians care nothing except about appetites. Your talks, they can wait. But what I ask is important. You will go?"

With her long hair brushing his bare chest from above, and his member in considerable ecstasy, Harold could not refuse. For that matter, with his mouth full of her bosom, he could not speak, and so despite misgivings he'd bussed the next day to shattered Sarajevo and then with phrase-book Serbo-Croatian made his way via tortuous land travel to arrive at the shrine by the crest of the hill upon which five teenagers swore the Virgin repeatedly appeared to them. He'd even jogged with hardly a protesting lung—at least he could still run, he complimented himself—to stand at the appointed place near an old church in this forsaken and muddy piece of Bosnia-Hercegovina, at the appointed eventide, to await Snezana's emissary. Shivering, listening to the babble of various tongues, Harold wondered if any sexual delight was worth this? If only his wife had loved him as had his amoeba! And what of his children, those mini-traitors who would rather have her and her consort? No miracle converted them to him. He, Harold

Fickleman, stood alone. The Amoeba Man. What an epitaph! Next to him an elderly pilgrim hacked and spat. The glob slid down Harold's left pant leg to his shoe. That's it, Harold thought. Screw this, I'm going someplace warm. Someplace normal. Harold turned, and felt his heart jump. There stood Maynard, his round face glistening again, this time with rain.

"You!" Harold blurted.

"Sorry, old chum. Took me a bit of time, too. Shall we go?"

The battered hotel in Sarajevo once held Olympians, but that had been a few years ago, so it was natural, Maynard said, that the wallboard seams should bulge, the shower function intermittently, and the telephone hiss like a cobra.

"Yugoslavs are great destroyers, not great builders," he said. "Except of course for the monasteries, and I must say they are beautiful, but at the earliest, eighth century. Anything else that lasted is Roman, and since the monks, well, not much, as you see . . ."

Maynard's lecturing style carried him from one side of the room to the next, past the windows where the dawn din of motorcycles and unmuffled trucks made Harold's ears ring, and toward the bureau on which sat several bottles of ghastly *konjak*. Two were empty, the contents unevenly split between them. Harold wished someone would answer the ringing in his ears, and then Maynard picked up the telephone.

"Da," he said. This he followed with unintelligible word spurts, a few more affirmatives, and a ringing *fala*.

"Who are you thanking for what?" Harold asked. "What's going on? Why don't we sleep? Why are we here? Are *you* the Virgin Mary?"

Maynard's smile split his round face like a jack-o-lantern's.

"Ah, the game's up, my new friend. Now you will see." Harold watched Maynard pull a leprous leather briefcase from the closet. The key twisted several times before the old flap lock released. Maynard's small pink hand descended into the fissured lips of the case and emerged holding what seemed to be a very old book.

"Behold, Harold Fickleman, your commission."

Harold gaped, but before he could respond, Maynard reached again into the case. This time he came up with what looked like a Styrofoam wienie.

"And the reason for the commission, Harold," Maynard intoned, advancing toward Fickleman. "Make no mistake, this is vital." Maynard slid into the chair across the table from Harold, putting both book and wienie down with great care. "It's this way," he began.

Harold scrutinized the dark, wolfish man two marble-topped tables away, sure that this was the one meant to kill him. He wiped his palms on his black cassock, then raised the ouzo to his lips. Damn the beard. Had to be horse hair, it itched so much. On the train down from Skopje he'd wanted to tear it off and toss it out a window but hadn't. Just as he hadn't refused any of this ridiculous charade. Fickleman looked again at the dark man. Had he penetrated this disguise? Did Orthodox priests always keep this silly chimney-like hat on? Harold hoped so. How ignominious, to die here in Thessaloniki, on the quay and be found out not as a man of God but as The Amoeba Man. Another sip of ouzo. Thank God Orthodox priests drank early and publicly. The dark man now looked out the window, across the bay and if he had good eyes across Thermaïkós Kólpos to Mt. Olympus. Harold relaxed, to go over again his commission, as odd in its way as when, amoeba-stricken, he had jogged himself invisible. Now, still amoeba-related, he sought a certain kind of visibility. But such a kind. The dark man stood now and moved into the sunlit door square, then out along the quay. Fickleman relaxed. Not much more now, until the bus to Ouranoupolis.

Inclining his stovepipe hat, he signaled for another ouzo.

The licorice-like liquid warmed his throat, just as Greece warmed his body. So different from the cold of Medagorje, the muddy trail to the Virgin's site. Different from Sarajevo's tormented modernity, too, and decidedly from the chilly intoxication of Skopje, lying in half-contemporary, half-medieval sprawl not two hundred miles up the Vardar valley from this bustling, jolly Greek metropolis. Harold folded his hands as if in silent prayer. Maynard was right. It kept the garrulous Thessalonikians from engaging him in conversation, a good thing since he knew little Latin and less Greek. Ah, Maynard, Maynard. What have you gotten me into? But then, Harold reminded himself, he'd come to this corner of the world seeking change, seeking solace just as his brother had, also in Greece. But by such a different path, it seemed. Fickleman, eyes closed, hands clasped, considered his path.

"You told me, did you not," Maynard had said in Sarajevo, "that you lack conviction and commitment?"

"I did?"

"Yes. The night of your arrival. In my flat."

"Oh."

"Yes. And so, too, did you tell Snezana."

"I did?"

"Yes. In her flat."

"Oh."

"Now, dear friend, to fix that."

And then, behind his closed lids, Harold saw again the book and the wienie. He heard again Maynard telling him the unbelievable, and felt himself somehow believing it again. All quite simple, Maynard said.

"This book, as you see it's a quite old missal written in Cyrillic, contains in cipher a recipe that certain Macedonian officials and businessmen would kill for. Yes, Fickleone, kill for, because as you may have deduced the production of wines and spiritous liquids is the largest industry in Macedonia, or at least the most profitable, and since the Macedonian, like any other Yugoslav, is a capitalist in sheared Marxist wool, they want to keep it that way. How else, dear friend, have they villas on the Adriatic, foreign exchange in their bank accounts, and mistresses in Italy? While the lumpenproletariat slave and suffer, of course."

"But," Harold had asked, "what does the recipe have to do with that, and any of it with me?" Unfortunately, Maynard had told him.

"First, imagine what a Marxist cutthroat capitalist could do with a drunk-making fungus that costs almost nothing to make? And then what if he could manipulate behavior by offering an antidote that costs equally little." Maynard's eyes became arrow slits. "Think of the private sales! Think of what he might get for it. Do you see?"

"Not yet," Harold had stammered. "And what's my role anyway?"

Maynard's sigh matched the opening of his blue eyes.

"Well, let's see. You know, dear one, the term *euroky*, of course?"

"Yes. The ability of an organism to live under variable environmental conditions."

"Like an amoeba, dear friend?"

"Yes, conceivably."

"That's Snezana's field, dear boy, and that's why you're involved, and me, and she, and the book, and this vial."

Then Maynard had spun out the whole tale. Even in dream-shimmery retrospect, the story stood rock-solid, a Gibralter of improbable fact, an oxymoronic lump in Fickleman's life. Maynard related how Snezana, the granddaughter of a priest slain in the Communist accession of World War II, discovered the book in her grandfather's pitiful pile of belongings and then, fearful for her life, hid it in the formerly defunct church in the wayside village of Medagorje. But with the teenagers' reports of the Blessed Virgin's appearance, she feared the church warders would find the volume behind the weeping statue of Christ. At first, Harold was to be the unwitting courier, but Maynard, a scholar of ancient texts, had ferreted out the existence of the missal himself, largely through bugging Snezana's flat. But then, Maynard said, they discovered they had much in common: a loathing for Tito's lackeys, especially the closet capitalists with their hands on the throats of the impoverished Macedonians. So, when Maynard cracked the crude Cyrillic cipher, they had a weapon: a fungus discovered in the tenth century that, when mixed with water, made people hilariously drunk. The monks, they learned, used it as the Mexicans used the magic mushroom, to become God's Fools, to cut through the veil of maya to the truth of the universe, in short, to cut the crap and see what was of value. Love and faith was the bottom line, Maynard said, and right then he and Snezana decided to return the secret to its owners, the Serbian monks now cloistered in the Holy Mountain Athos in the chalkidiki of Greece. Two huge problems beset the conspirators, though. First, they learned that the ancient monks had no remedy for the intoxication.

"So," Maynard said, "Snezana brewed up a batch of the stuff, analyzed it, and after a few weeks' work developed a strain of amoeba that would devour the fungus. That's what's in the vial."

The second problem loomed larger now and accounted for Harold's disguised role.

"Really," Maynard recalled, "just after Snezana got the cure, the bastards found me out. I was close to death. The Kavardaki vintners got wind of me somehow, only me, thank God, and bugged *me*. Can you imagine? I barely escaped one night by feigning sexual congress with dear Snezana. The poor stupid hit man didn't want to dispatch a man *in flagrante delicto*, so he left. I departed, too, to cool off in Belgrade, and then, like a miracle, I encountered you on the way back to resume the game."

"And the two of you decided to use me."

"Yes, but Snezana truly liked you anyway. Surely you believe that."

Sipping his ouzo now, Father Fickleman could not dispute Maynard. After Sarajevo, they'd traveled in Maynard's rented car over daunting mountains back to Skopje. Maynard rattled on about injustice, about his half-Italian heritage, his "true Communist" father, and his consequent devotion to the poor, and about his days in MI-5, and about Mt. Athos, how anomalous it was, a community of monks in scattered monasteries who ruled themselves and had allowed no females onto their peninsula for a thousand years. Not even female animals. Maynard marveled, how strange and yet interesting that must be! Harold did fill with wonder, but mainly at his situation. He'd gone from invisible jogger to farcical conspirator, and to pondering an eternal question: what is good intoxication, and what bad? To be sure, in Skopje he next felt another splendid erotic intoxication. Snezana showed him avenues of ecstasy, and of affection, that he had never trod. Harold felt loved, or so that feeling must be, he realized there in the bar at Thessaloniki, realizing, too, that recently he hadn't once thought of his lost wife and children, not even when in the station bathroom at Thessaloniki he'd donned his priest's garb, stowed the missal and vial in a black leather attaché case, and set off to wait for his bus. But after his courier's job, what?

Harold opened his eyes to the large clock above the marble bar. Eight A.M. Time to walk for the bus. Then what, indeed? For the first time in a very long time he didn't need an answer. He would deliver the goods and then worry about what came next. Fickleman took a final sip. What would it be like, after all, to be perpetually drunk? Lord, he'd save money, probably ruining a few distillers all by himself. He felt the tall, narrow glass slide from his grasp. My God, he sat there afire with apprehension, with desire. An image of Snezana flashed before him, spread on the bed, and then one of Maynard handing up his costume and papers and attaché case while waving good-bye at the night train in Skopje, and then he realized he was trembling with tense joy, like that he'd felt at the end of a particularly good run. He set the glass upright, and in his robes stiff-legged it toward the door, out and up the hill toward *Platia Omonias.*

Father Fickleman's sides were wet with sweat, and not only from the stifling bus, now rattling in its final throes from Ierissos toward Ouranoupolis. He'd sat, clutching his case, in an extremis of fear ever since midway in the noisy, hot, three-hour journey when, at Palaiokastron, the wolfish man of the quayside bar boarded the bus. Harold's back itched, as if a target's concentric circles were tattooed there. Worse, he wasn't certain what to do. Maynard's instructions simply had him walking from the bus stop to the gate barring entrance to the sacred peninsula, showing the special pilgrim's papers, and sauntering in. But with the wolf in pursuit, what to do?

He saw the bus had come into Ouranoupolis itself: the pastel and white Greek houses, the pitted asphalt road, the signs of tobacconists and tavernas, the onion-domed churches. They'd make for the waterfront, of course, because normal male visitors to Mt. Athos took the ferry down the coast to Dafni. An august divine like Fickleman, however, could use the land route, walking like John the Baptist to the chosen rendezvous. Oh, no, not like John the Baptist. Hadn't he lost his head? There, there was the water!

Fickleman stood, and with him the fellow passengers, everyone flailing with parcels, shopping bags, battered luggage, as in a babble of voices they boiled toward the exit. Harold saw the wolfish man trapped near the rear. With unpriestly rudeness he pushed through to the door, noting that, reluctantly and with what sounded like curses, the Greeks made way for the holy man. The pneumatic whoosh opened the door, and Fickleman dropped onto the pavement. Near the ferry entrance, highlighted by the afternoon sun off the Aegean, stood a policeman. Fickleman ran to him.

"Athos! Athos!" he shouted.

The Greek stared at him, at this frantic priest obviously in a paroxysm of devotion, shrugged, and pointed toward a street angling inland from the port. Fickleman nodded, his stovepipe hat bobbing, and took off jogging. He saw behind him the wolf settle into a run, too.

Fickleman ran past the houses, through the clots of villagers amazed at the holy marathoner, pounding past them with his skirt clutched waist-high, his beard bobbing. Harold ran uphill, taking the middle of the street, dodging the cars and trucks, fishing for breath and cursing his recent dissolute ways. After a quarter-mile he could see the end of the street and not much farther on, a kiosk beside a fence, and the gate. He picked up the pace, looking back to find the wolfish man, who seemed to have lost ground. Harold could barely make out the strained face, but it seemed set and determined. Fickleman ran on, and as he cleared the last house he felt the endorphins click in. God, he was runner-drunk, and he ran faster. Now his pursuer was a stick figure, still in the street of the village. Fickleman felt invisible again, exalted, and he pounded on until, reluctantly, he stopped at the kiosk. He clicked open the attaché case. He thrust his permits at the dumbfounded guard, who muttered, scanned the papers, then went into the kiosk. The wolfish man labored on, a scant four hundred yards away. Harold heard the comforting thump of a rubber stamp, and then the guard was back, holding out the papers.

"*Efhersito,*" said Harold, in one of his three Greek words. The guard raised the red-and-white gate pole, and Fickleman sprinted into Mt. Athos. From a copse of olive trees a few hundred yards from the border, he saw the wolfish man shouting, gesticulating, at the guard, then turn and with bent shoulders walk back toward Ouranoupolis. Sanctuary! Harold allowed himself a smile, allowed himself a brief rest, allowed his muscles to relax. Then, Maynard's map in hand, he stepped off for the holy monastery of Hiliandariou, four miles away over the lower ridge of the sacred mountain.

Near dusk, Fickleman staggered into the monastery's grounds. Its size surprised him. Although Maynard's lecture told him only fifteen Serbian monks permanently inhabited the place, it stretched long and wide in the forested valley. True, many holy men and simple pilgrims visited to be reborn, for that was the Abbey's claim: to give rebirth to faith. Harold stared at his map, orienting it with the monastery's buildings. There! The little building to the southwest, with a gallery of windows and a small onion dome. That's where he was to meet his contact and at last rid himself of the missal, the vial, his robes, his beard, his falsity. Thank the Lord.

Fickleman knocked the prescribed three times ("sacred number, don't you know," Maynard's canard went). The sound boomed, and Harold felt the silence of this place, as he'd felt the silence of the path along which he'd walked. Maybe these monks had something. A man could think and feel here, probably, and that certainly could be a rebirth. The weathered wooden door swung open. A cowled, bearded face stared at him.

"Da?"

"Yas sum Fickleman."

The beard split into a laugh, and the cowl went flying back even as Harold was pulled into the half-light of the building.

"Of course, you are, dear boy. Welcome!" Maynard's laugh reverberated in the stone halls, up to the dome, and Fickleman saw pigeons take flight.

"Well done, Harold. Well done. You've made the world safe from greedy distillers. Come with me."

Fickleman followed, dazed and tired, up a stone staircase into a large bedchamber. He saw his luggage stacked neatly against the far wall. A hearth fire cast shadows over the room, brightly enough lit by candles. Another robed figure sat hunched at the desk.

"Now, my friend, the goods."

Harold handed over the case. Maynard took the missal and vial and papers.

"Fickleone, these have found their proper home. I, too, have. Do you know they have over 780 codes of ancient Slavic manuscripts untranslated? But what of you?"

"I don't know."

The second monk rose and came toward Harold, the cowl shadowing the face.

"But I do." The monk threw back the hood, and Harold saw but could not quite believe it. Snezana!

"Now, Fickleman," she said. "Starting here, we will maybe drink the fungus and proceed then to frolic. We will maybe drink the amoebas, and then, no matter, God's fools, eh?" Maynard sidled out the door. Harold saw he'd left a chalice by the candle on the bedside table.

"Maybe," Harold managed, but without full conviction, even after they'd struggled out of the robes. Euroky was so difficult, as every Amoebae Man knew.

# The Ficklemen Figure It Out

Harold Fickleman held his brother Henry's letter as if it were a grain of plutonium—gingerly, with the sure sense that it had doomed him. Not since he had departed the pseudo-monastic life of Mt. Athos—what goats those monks were, with animals, boys, and smuggled women!—had he felt a more destinal moment. To tell the truth, it felt good. This suspended atmosphere he'd found and cherished in Greece had by now evaporated in the stale heat of placid everyday life. Now, Henry's letter, the first he'd received since they'd each self- and other-destructed, came bearing as much force as that first moment when Harold's pet amoeba at last divided.

He read:

> Brother Harold (for I can so address you, the monks of Mt. Athos notwithstanding):

I hope this reaches you in your remote lair. No doubt you are having it off with single-celled creatures or running your body and soul into the ground with abstruse reasoning, bizarre and unsought plots or worse, aerobics.

Well, I plan to save you from such ill-starred pastimes (and haven't we each had a bunch of those lately?). I can't tell you all the details, but be assured they will accommodate our different and similar interests. It involves travel, of course, but our current professions are both portable, eh?

So, meet me in two weeks' time at the Hotel Delfin in poor old Dubrovnik, formerly Ragusa, as my new Italian friends tell me. I'll be wearing a carnation. That's a joke, Harold. You'll recognize me, I hope, not least from the forehead scar you inflicted when you threw your microscope at me when I gently suggested that a ten-year-old could not hope to solve the problem of protozoan origins after school and before supper. Remember? Worse, you compounded the injury by pin pricking the condom I carried in my wallet. No wonder I reported to our late, unlamented parents that you exhibited a tendency towards eroticism and slimy fluids.

Anyway, dear found-again brother, meet me at the Delfin.

Your brother,

Henry

P.S. If you're wondering how I got your address, it came from your estranged wife, who had it wangled by the State Dept. from some doxie you met in Yugoland. The trails we leave, like slugs. Ciao.

Harold examined the envelope. Postmarked Napoli, Italy. He sniffed it. It smelled of a sea breeze, like the tissue he often took to his nose on the ferry when the wind made his sinuses run. Pushing open the louvered doors, he edged onto the meter-wide balcony that hung like an afterthought from this new, old-looking tourist hotel. Straight below were the awnings shading the hotel's cafe. Bursts of Greek shot up to him. A hundred meters down this beachfront street lined with tourist shops lay the quay, empty now. The next ferry from the mainland wasn't due for a half-hour. Harold liked to watch the boats come and go. The natives of Thassos didn't show much excitement. So, Feeklemon, another boat. So? But it thrilled Harold to know that he was islanded, and that he had a way off if he wanted, needed it. Today, though, the quay sat empty except for some boys booting a soccer ball from end to end of the wharf. Harold stared north and east toward ancient Alexandropolis, whence Alexander's fleet had embarked for Persia. He looked northwest next, toward Kavala and the plains of Phillipi, and beyond that, Drama, where all the world *was* a stage. He liked to think perhaps some grandeur reflected back to him, but when he turned to the whitewashed room, furnished with pressed-wood wardrobe, cheap nightstand, pipe-metal bed, he felt with somatic certainty that he was merely a self-exiled speck sitting on another speck on a sea that had lost its significance centuries ago. Still, specks had to move. Even amoebae moved. Harold began to pack his few things. Why not Dubrovnik? Another sea, another change. Folding up his running suit, he was struck by the past, and he fell back into it, as if that spot on time's continuum were a black hole.

Henry Fickleman regarded his old white La Coste shirt. Except for one tiny ballpoint inkstain, it looked OK. He even looked OK in it, if he sucked in his modest paunch. Should be fine for Dubrovnik, itself now stained.

Harold would show, Henry knew. His brother was nothing if not reliable, even in his occasional unreliability. All those years when Henry was screwing around and screwing up his life in the process, Reliable Harold worked away, worked at his job, worked at his marriage, took off weight running his sorrows into the pavement, even worked at getting his amoeba to divide. Sweet Harold. Henry thrust his last pair of socks into the canvas airline bag. Sweet Harold. Sour Henry. Lord, how they had turned out, although Harold's recent past with the Yugo and Greek capers had, Henry thought, moved Harold closer in spirit to him. He'd see.

Henry picked up the telephone. "Si, Signore," came the tinny voice. "Per piacere," Henry said. "Auto por Signore Fickleman. Grazie." "Si, Signore," said the voice. Henry hoisted his bag. Grande villas had their amenities, and he must remember to thank Constantina for her hospitality. He'd leave a note. She never rose before three in the afternoon. But then, she stayed up until five in the morning. Odd, wasn't it, that for all her money and sophistication, she was so desperately unhappy, willing to take in any male with a modicum of good manners and an active libido. Well, good for her, certainly good for Henry. He stepped into the marble-floored hallway, then down it to the small elevator. On the veranda, Henry inhaled the warm morning air, drawing in the aroma of unearned riches, and then ducked into the Jaguar. "A aeropuerto," he mumbled. The car crunched the oyster-shell drive. When it passed the stone eagles atop the pedestals marking the driveway (vive il Duce! Henry thought) he turned to wave goodbye to the slumbering Constantina, bless her open thighs and purse. He'd always been lucky with a certain kind of woman, a luck which was itself often unlucky. Dear, depraved Thelma came to mind, and Edna of the airplanes. Constantina was of a different stripe, slightly. American-born of Italian parents, she was upper-middle-class enough to learn good manners combined with a rebellious air that gave women of that stratum a certain smoky sexiness. That's how she'd snared Count Dominick Castelli, who passed his time calculating Fiat and other high-lira dividends over gaming tables around the world. Dominick spent millions, but he had them, and he was seldom at home. When he was, he usually was accompanied. During Henry's stay, his tag-along was a sweet Thai-French girl named Monique, at least that's what Henry remembered from the once he'd met the villa's master. Meanwhile, Constantina picked up lovers like other women picked up vegetables at the market. She inspected them, pinched them, finally ate them alive. Henry had been her sixth of the year, she'd said, or one a month. But God help him, she was Olympic class in bed, and far from stingy. Of course, she wouldn't know just how generous she'd been until the charges arrived from the credit cards Henry liberated from Dominick's wing of Villa Castelli while the great gambler was gamboling in the sunken tub with Monique. A trifle unethical, Henry admitted, but then he'd rendered Constantina very good service. Besides, how else was he to finance this Dubrovnik ploy?

Surprisingly enough, the JAT airliner stood ready to depart. Henry's flying days had taught him the rarity of that. Of course, most East European lines were worse. His old flying pal Ernie Butcher once had spent five days on Aeroflot trying to get from Minsk to Moscow, and that was with good weather. The troubles were fuel, flight controlers, and fights between Ukranian authorities and Muscovites, according to Ernie. Henry wondered how Ernie was doing. A shame Constantina had gotten between them and their flying service, but Ernie was probably all right, flying along a hundred feet above pipelines looking for breaks and sabotage. Good money, and when Ernie needed booze and broads, which was often, Cairo was close. Henry got off the transit bus with the few tense Dubrovnik-bound passengers in time to wave again at the Jaguar, still nosed against the chain-link of the Naples airport. Pietro waved back and shrugged. He'd been the closest thing Henry had to a friend in Villa Castelli. When the Signora was away getting her fingernails glued on and her wrinkles smoothed, Pietro and Henry drank Strega and coffee in town. Pietro, in fact, was Henry's confidant. Nine this year, he said, not six. Pietro, too, led Henry to the credit cards Dominick always left at home so his expenses couldn't be traced, and it was Pietro who knew about the foreign-exchange account the Castellis kept in Dubrovnik. Henry waved again from the top of the staircase before he ducked into the DC-9.

The flight would take an hour, Henry knew. After the teeth-rattling charge down the runway, and the surge for altitude, he relaxed into the seat, waving away the scowling Croatian flight attendant with her paper container of orange juice. So, he'd soon see Harold again, and what would he think of that, and for that matter, what would Harold think of it all? Henry studied the calm blue sea below, until a wisp of white cloud washed over it and turned his mind to other things, other times.

"So, Feeklemon, you is leave? Here is Kavala, if you is leave." Harold took the tissue from his nose to look at Nikos. He hadn't made that many trips to the mainland since fetching up at Thassos, but this genial, overfed Greed had steered the ferry on every one. Today, this early, Nikos glowed as if lit by noon sunlight, even though old sol was barely above the eastern horizon.

"Yes, I've got to go, Nikos. Dubrovnik. Have to meet my brother. Family."

"Ah-ho, Feeklemon. Family best important. I have sixty brother."

Harold smiled and nodded. Nikos surely meant six brothers, but so what? He took Nikos' hand and pumped vigorously.

"Best important is right. Sometimes anyway."

Nikos grinned then turned his attention to guiding the ferry into the slip, dodging the fishing boats going and coming, and the other ferries setting out. When the hawsers had been made fast, Nikos wheeled to Harold.

"Take careful, Feeklemon," he blurted. "Slavs is dangerous."

"I know, Nikos," Harold said, and then as the ramp went down and the trucks coughed into life, he bussed Nikos on the cheeks. "Adio," he murmured and followed the passengers and vehicles onto the Kavala quay. His bus to Thessaloniki left soon, and then there was the afternoon train back up to Skopje, where Harold's Mt. Athos misadventure had begun. He'd lay over in the bus station there, thankful that in this fine weather he could nap outside the fetid terminal, and make the morning bus for Dubrovnik. God and checkpoints willing he should be there late tomorrow evening. Harold dropped his bag and backpack on the bus stop's bench. He felt relaxed, but anticipatory and, for no reason, good and healthy. A young Greek mother, with a garlicky toddler in tow, dropped down beside him, she chattering happily to the boy. Harold thought of his own children and without the gag-reflex guilt he usually endured when he let his mind go to them and their mother.

Henry's cloudy memories swirled in him like the cream in his coffee, light streaks against the black of what must be his inner soul. What else could it be, this dark thing at his center? Sure, he'd been told often enough, and told himself often enough, that his life for the past few years had been blighted by some dark character flaw. There had been the crazed affair with Thelma, and his escape from her into a succession of surrogate sybarites. Some escape.

There had been his excesses, the binge drinking that excited, exalted him as long as it lasted, only to crash land him in the desert of despair when it ended. Of course, he always took wing again. There was no shortage of ethanol fuel in the world. There'd been the travel, carrying his spotted self around as if it were a body in his garment bag to be returned home for reburial. Trouble was, he hadn't felt at home anywhere. Hadn't felt at home since he'd left what he then felt was his suburban hell and took up with Thelma. Thinking of whom, he wondered how her flying evangelist business was getting on and whether she was still with Barney Malafort, the Rock of Righteousness. Maybe Thelma had changed her name to fit the business. To something Biblical like Tamar, although Henry could not imagine anyone having to force Thelma to have sex, as Annon had forced David's daughter. Wasn't the Bible a hoot, though, all full of behavior it counseled against? Well, that made it lifelike. And Thelma and Barney, like old Ernie Butcher, were no doubt making money while Henry was down to his last few hundred dollars and several thousand lira. But, on the bright side, he had resources and was headed for a reunion. He glanced out the starboard window, then wrenched his eyes forward. No time for feeling now, no time to think that somewhere down there his brother was making his way back to him, or that his wife and her lover, and her children, were settling down to a long Greek lunch, hearing that old Adriatic rag wash on Corfu's shores. Henry's eyes teared. He wiped their corners, as surreptitiously as possible, the way he did in sentimental movies, and told himself again that he was more than that dark soul spot. His blemish was surrounded with something of a lighter hue, like these clouds through which they were descending toward the landing at Dubrovnik, he and his fellow travelers, each freighting their burdens, hopes, fears, plans.

The man hawking the basket of passports pushed past Harold just in advance of the bus conductor. "Papers, papers, cheap, cheap," he chirped in Greek, German, English, French, and Turkish. Harold knew him as a regular feature on the run from Kavala to Thessaloniki. Another like him haunted the train that ran north from Greece, but that one inserted Serbian in his litany of languages. The conductor tore Harold's ticket, grunted *efharisto,* and moved on. Harold returned to the daydream of his children. They would be bigger now, maybe big and old enough to understand why their father had run away into himself, or even to fathom why their mother could no longer stand living with a man who had prized an amoeba above her. Harold sighed at the thought. But then lives are continua of disynchronous events. When one person is ready for something, the other usually isn't, and so it goes. He stared at the bright mirrors of the small lakes the bus jolted past. Like new coins, although they had names, Volvi and Koronia. The young mother from Kavala was pointing them out to her son. Harold saw his own son then in the mirror of his mind, small and eager for knowledge, and his daughter, lanky and now just entering womanhood, smarting for the sting of experience. It had been a Greek, hadn't it—Aristotle—who'd said humans are by nature curious, and so the trick of education was to teach them what would be most valuable to them? For Harold it had been the running's endorphins, amoebae, the travel, that had taught him he was ready, finally, to learn something. The bus now was in the traffic that fed into the main road from the three fingers of the chaldiki. Harold listened to the clatter, the high Greek voices rattling in the bus, felt the mid-morning sun's heat. He dozed, not to come full awake until the bus bumped its way into Thessaloniki's Agias Sofias boulevard, headed for the bus terminal. From there it was a short walk to the railway station, and he had ample time.

The coach pulled nearly onto the walkway fronting the Hotel Delfin, the driver yelping wildly to his passengers that they were arrived here. Henry released the arm grips gratefully. The ride to Dubrovnik, or at least to the new part of the ancient city, had harrowed him more than the hop across Italy and the Adriatic. So much damage. So? He checked his watch. Three P.M. Why Constantina would even now be rising from her satin sheets, finding his so-sorry note, and beginning her four-hour toilette. She might curse for a moment, he thought, but then would call for Angelina to fetch her Rolodex and that would be the end of Henry Fickleman. Or so she thought.

The Delfin's lobby echoed to Henry's footsteps and those of the other foreigners who would stay in what the government called a grand international hotel. Foreigners would be about the only ones to stay there, and at a hefty hard-currency price. Yugoslavs might stay and at a lower rate, but few did because even the lower rate, paid in worthless dinars, was more than most could afford. Henry didn't have a worry, however. He had Dominick's cards. A German couple who'd ridden in with him from the airport moved from the desk, following their bellhop. The clerk beamed as Henry slapped the BancaSuissa VISA plastic on the marble desk, saying in his clearest English, "I'd like a high, safe room, please, a suite if you have one."

They did. A burly Bosnian led Henry through the Venetian-styled lobby, all pink marble, brassy gold, and green-patina flambeaus, to a bank of elevators. Amazingly, one came a moment after being summoned. Henry entered the traveling cubicle. It smelled of cigarettes, rose attar, and sweat. Laboriously, the car began its climb.

"Bella, bellissimo," bleated the Bosnian, waving at the car, which hideously enough was also pink-marbled and flam-beaued.

"Yes, very pretty," Henry said.

"Ah, angliski!" boomed the Bosnian.

"Amerikanski," Henry said. "I live in Italy." The man bowed. Henry saw visions of dollars dancing in the Bosnian's head. The elevator slammed to a stop, throwing Henry's carry-on bag back against the bellhop. "Son-bitch," he squealed and smiled, gesturing that Henry should de-car.

The short corridor had only two doors, one at each end. Henry's escort led him to the left one, adorned with a brass dolphin knocker. "Here, Signor Castelli, the life of a Tito!" Henry's eyes roamed, from the solid glass and its terrace beyond out over the old walled city to the blue-gray Aegean dancing in the late-afternoon sun. He saw the living room with three sofas facing the windows, and there was the wet bar and kitchen along the right rear wall, and the open doors to the four bedrooms, two to each end of the suite. The bellhop pushed open a door between two bedrooms. The sunken bath looked big enough to float a car ferry, and there was a shower stall, two vanities, heated towel racks, and a commode fit, yes, for an ass as big as Tito's.

"Another there," the bellhop said, pointing across the plush carpet to the suite's other end.

"Bellissimo," Henry said, stuffing a handful of lira into the bellhop's hands. The man bowed again and, fingering the hard-currency bank notes, backed out the entry door. The door shut with a solid clunk. Henry bolted it before stepping to the Euromodel telephone set on the parquet coffee table. The numbers he knew by heart he hoped had not changed. The others he'd have to have help with. Henry started to dial.

Harold's body ached as if it had been beaten instead of merely deposited on the ground for a night of restless sleep. He stretched again, peering past the bridge over the Vardar where the Turks had, not all that many decades ago, hung living Slavs on pikes as a reminder to passersby that revolt was dangerous. Skopje's sounds, familiar enough, rocked the early morning air: motorbikes, roaring trucks, the Albanians' iron-rimmed handcarts, the shouts of flower and food vendors, the cough-cough of the Zastavas, and under it all the murmur of voices, disputing, consoling, bargaining, gossiping, the voices of a city in full cry. Harold breathed in the sweet-stingy diesel of a bus pulling out. His watch testified to 7:00 A.M. Two hours before his bus headed for Dubrovnik. Time for a pastry, a coffee, and maybe something else. Harold hauled himself, then his luggage, up and started off on complaining knees for the *kafane* of the *stare grad,* the old Turkish quarter.

Harold joined the crowd coming off the bridge into the corkscrew streets of the bazaar. The thoroughly Western Slavs slouched along in ill-fitting suits, trailing clouds of strong, black tobacco smoke. Harold remembered all too well his previous brief stay in Skopje amongst those cynical sinecure-holders whose allegiance to socialism was as thin as their commitment to the unvarnished truth. He thought back to Snezana and Maynard and their scam, and to his deluded notions of eventual happiness. As for euroky, Harold supposed he had achieved that. Surely he'd adapted to variable conditions, most certainly in his doomed stay on Mt. Athos, unhappily, and his recovery on Thassos, contentedly. But happiness? That was for others, and besides, he didn't trust it. Nothing lasts, as his and Henry's grandmother had said, so happiness even if achieved would go, to be replaced by misery, which in turn would be succeeded by something else, and so on. All one could hope for was to die in a pleasant cycle. That thought drove his synapses, quite involuntarily, to Snezana. Con-lady she might have been, but she'd taught him pleasure, if not happiness, taught him leap and twist, physical and mental, counter-leap and counter-twist. A shame it had all been in the interest of caper and counter-caper, but so it had gone. Harold shrugged away the vaporous regret, hoping his infant erection would subside, too.

He jostled now amongst more interesting folks. The Slavs dispersed into their party-secured offices and businesses, leaving the raw, aromatic areas of life to these voluble Albanians and Turks, pressing around him and into the *bifes,* tea glasses in hand, sweet pastry crumbs speckling their moustaches. He scanned the faces, hoping not to see Maynard the Conspirator who, in Harold's now sober memory, ranked with Vlad the Impaler. Except that Maynard had impaled Harold on the pikes of lust and greed. Not that Fickleman, Harold, had not greatly enjoyed the favors of Snezana, all the sweeter for having them granted in the all-male world of Mt. Athos. Nor had Harold greatly regretted transporting the Fungus of Bliss to the Sacred Mountain. So far as he knew, it was still safely there, away from the wicked ways of capitalists, or at least unchurched capitalists. In his stay with the monks, after Snezana's mysterious disappearance one night, Harold had tried the fungus' product. The high was like that of running, a sort of heart-pounding rush, then an elevation, painless and quick, to a point from which in perfect joy one could contemplate the world's misery. The drawback was the descent, equally quick, but painless except to a soul returning to banality.

Now, with a *kolace* in front of him, and a strong Turkish coffee, Harold could give thanks he'd mustered the guts to leave Athos, leave Maynard to hatch his schemes on behalf of the Athos monks, who in their monastery v. monastery intrigues resembled nothing so much as an Unholy Roman and Orthodox Empire. When he'd left, the Serbian monks had been planning an amphibious raid on the Russian monkhouse to recover an icon supposedly lifted from Serbia in the eighteenth century. Yes, Harold decided, he'd much rather be here watching hundreds of cabbages roll off an Albanian's cart than sitting on Athos, or for that matter chilling out in his hotel in Thassos. And his erotic flush over Snezana was gone. He clumped a handful of dinars on the table then ushered himself into the stream of people headed back toward the bridge and his bus. He avoided looking at the families, concentrating instead on what in hell or earth Henry might really want, and on the odor of roasting chestnuts ascending like the souls of saints above the onion domes of the Orthodox *crkve*.

The oyster lay gray, slimy, and gorgeous in the pearly shell. Henry raised it to his back-tilted head then tipped the gnarled shell toward his gaped mouth. The liquor, salt and sweet, poured down his throat. He imagined it to be the sea's semen. Then like a tentacle the shellfish slithered in and his jaws closed on it. A slug by any other name, but my, how good it tasted, fresh out of the Adriatic. Henry took a mighty swallow of acid white wine, Domestica. He and Ernie had guzzled some on Corfu, the late night of the evening he'd found his wife and her lover and his children in the village by the late Durrell's house. So much Domestica had he taken that Ernie finally eighty-sixed him with a short, swift punch to the temple. He'd slept until their plane was over Brindisi. His head throbbed for two days after Ernie had deposited him with Constantina. Of course, Ernie had known her when she'd just been Angela Costello back in Kansas City, a teenage skydiver and water-skier who'd specialized in ski-gliding behind Ernie's seaplane on the Lake of the Ozarks. Quite a progression from that to her current high-flying. Henry fingered Dominick's credit cards. Here, centered in the ancient square of ancient Dubrovnik, a showcase city, blessed with goods and tourist spots still, Henry could hear the Adriatic slapping the sea wall and he could charge these wonderful oysters to Dominick. Outside vendors hawked leather goods, small pieces of furniture, vegetables, slav-made Black & Decker tools. Their cries echoed off the three churches hulking around the plaza. Now they were for worshippers as well as tourists, and on this Sunday morning he could hear, counterpointing the sea, a single voice raised in high, Gregorian Orthodox chant. A pity Harold hadn't yet arrived, he thought, since he'd doubtless be able to place it. Henry tried to calculate Harold's possible arrival time, a task only partly impeded by more oysters and wine. The precise time wasn't crucial, exactly, but he should be able to guess within a day or so. Henry slurped the last of his oysters, the last of the wine, and signed the Diner's Club chit with a flourish. The waiter gave a distinct bow, but then the Italian influence was still strong here, even if Mussolini wasn't exactly a regional favorite.

Henry pushed into the square. The babble wrapped him like a receiving blanket and, for a moment, his mental slide projector threw an image of his quondam family into sharp image, but he shoved it away with a big brown bottle of *pivo* secured from a stand hard against the sea-wall church. He would wander the walls now, he decided, walk around the old city, beer in hand, and look down upon its red-tiled roofs and imagine the triremes, then the great high-pooped men-of-war circling the promontory, firing into it, seeking subjugation. Actually a sexual sort of image, he thought, the great egg of old Dubrovnik under bombardment through the ages. He took the nearest wall stairs two at a time. He wasn't the kind of runner Harold had once been, but Henry tried to stay in shape for whatever sports might come his way. On the wall's walkway the inshore breeze chilled, but a brisk pace put him warm again. The midday sun threw the city into relief below him, cast crosses on walls from the many churches. The diligent citizens plying the narrow paths seemed so many scurrying irrelevancies. No wonder God was so removed and arrogant, He had a much better view. Off to the south Henry saw the small-boat harbor clogged with blue-and-red fishing vessels, white-hulled sailboats, tern-gray motor cruisers. All carefully parked, with a nice corridor at the seaward end, protected by the towers that faced the Adriatic as the ancient line of defense. That would be just right, Henry saw. He continued his walk, whistling, and feeling the power of the oysters surging in him. He spied a flower vendor waving bouquets below and marveled at the availability of carnations.

To Harold, strategically seated on the seaward side of the bus, the intact roofs of Dubrovnik, ochre in the late sun, looked like red-pepper jelly spread across the beige granite slabs of the old city. Which reminded him he was hungry. And mortally weary of the jostling. He didn't know Dubrovnik but assumed the bus station would be in the near outskirts, as close to the old city as could be managed. He hoped so, because inasmuch as they now were negotiating a road hard by the outer walls, that meant they would soon enough be stopped, the kidney-pounding would cease, and he could seek rest, relief from the grinding over-the-mountains, through-the-woods, fourteen-hour passage from Skopje, during which he'd seen more run-down villages and slack, defeated people than he'd ever dreamed were extant. Sullenness was all, even in Titograd where, before Josip Broz Tito's eponymity took hold, the Kings and Princes of Montenegro held splendid Slavic fetes in Podgorica. Harold giggled at the thought of Tito, that great block of a man, horny as a goat, evading Nazis by day and shagging mountain peasant girls by night. Well, at least there was a leader with both death and life active in him. For that matter, even the dull gray statues of Tito they'd jolted past showed more life than Harold had recently felt. The bus abruptly braked. At the signal, his fellow travelers scrambled up, clawing for their belongings, grunting to the driver and themselves. Harold clutched his bag and waited until everyone debussed before coming down the shaky metal steps into the soft dusk. The sea smelled different here. Somehow rawer, newer, with a winey edge missing from the Aegean. Around him the passengers scattered, some embracing relatives and friends, some legging for the taxi stand. Harold noticed the signs, all in Latin lettering, not the cyrillic of Macedonia. The bus stand, he saw, lay across the street from a beach, and down that street, toward the old walls, he made out the Hotel Delfin's logo, black letters against the illuminated yellow favored by international hotel builders. Harold strode toward it, up the gradual slope. International hotel builders liked rooms with views, and Harold hoped Henry had one. Shifting his bag to his sinister hand, Harold pushed open the aluminum-framed doors with the hotel's gaudy crest wrought thereon in gold paint.

The Bosnian's beryl-blue jacket bore the same crest, a D entwined with waves, dolphins, and what looked like water nymphs.

"You another Americanski, same as other Feeklemon?" The man's voice resonating in the elevator rattled Harold's spectacles.

"Da."

"You live in Italy, also?"

"No. In Greece."

"Grcka? Good place, lots of money and food. I have cousin there. Here is your stop."

The doors whooshed open and the Bosnian led Harold to the suite's door. With a great flourish he hammered the dolphin knocker and, hearing nothing in five seconds, unlocked the door. With baronial manner—Harold had not seen such a flourish since Maynard—the bellman swung the door inward and waved at the luxurious expanse, which at the moment included two naked figures, caught as on a Greek frieze, the male just clambering over the back of the center of the three sofas, the female posed against the window, a carnation behind each ear.

"Henry!" cried Harold.

"Harold!" cried Henry.

"Bellissima!" cried the Bosnian.

"Excuse, please," said the girl, pelting for the nearer bedroom door. Instinctively, Harold turned to the bellman to press dinars into his hand then press him through the door. The slam cut off the stream of exclamations. Harold whirled to Henry, but Henry already was in full speech.

"Harold, Harold! My Lucifer! After all this time, it's wonderful to see you." Harold watched in something akin to wonder as Henry wriggled into undershorts that resembled a string bikini. Italian, no doubt.

"Nice to see all of you, too," said Harold. "Who's the girl?"

He wanted to say more, but Henry had vaulted the sofa, rushed to him, and embraced him so Harold could hardly breathe. He could smell, however, and his brother's breath reeked of *lozovaca*, a.k.a. *loza*, a particularly powerful grape brandy favored by the derelict class that under the beneficences of socialism shouldn't exist.

"Don't know her name. Lovely girl. Sells flowers. Met her in the old city. Goddam! it's great that you came."

Henry released Harold and stepped back, hoping his brother's fondness for analysis wouldn't come into play just now. Henry needed time for it all to unfold.

"Just great," Henry repeated. "How was Greece? Any fun? Any amoebae?" He removed his trousers hanging on the dolphin-based lamp and stepped into them.

"Millions, but I didn't study them," Harold said, evenly. "Actually I found flora and flora girls more interesting."

"Dovidjenja!" the girl blurted, bolting from the bedroom toward the door. Then she was gone in a billow of polyester, no longer a nymph, just a flower girl gone wrong. The Ficklemen stood looking at the closed door.

"Well," they said, simultaneously, and then they hugged again, shyly, like adolescents wanting to touch but afraid, and then they separated to slump into chairs and talk, occasionally laugh, about their former lives and wives, about growing up, the Christmases and model-building and tree houses and their dead parents, until finally tired of nostalgia they stood side-by-side at the windows drinking. By now the moon was up and the wall stood like a bright silver girdle around old Dubrovnik.

"So," Harold asked at last, "what's the plan to save me from my 'ill-starred' pastimes?"

Henry smiled. "Oh, brother, you always did tend to read things too closely."

"You wrote me this. I came. Now?"

Henry jolted down his kerosenish *vinjak*, Harold saw, as he had milk back before their worlds went wacky. Harold gulped his wine. He watched his brother form the words.

"All right. All right. Let's walk and talk."

The water jetted from beneath the dolphin's tail and torso, from under the creature's mouth and around its bottle-nose, up over the boy's upward-straining body, up in cascading fountains that in the night's light breeze blew into a fine spray that, caught in the bright-blue lights surrounding the fountain, looked to Harold Fickleman like diamonds blown from a dandelion stem. Henry Fickleman wiped the spray from his nose, wondering what his brother saw.

"So," said Henry, "what make you of the delphinida and the underage jockey?"

"I guess first the story," Harold replied. "Princes, weren't they, little princes like Theseus, protected by the dolphins or porpoises, and . . . "

"And," Henry interrupted, "they didn't just protect the young men, who by the way were all icons of Pallas, a word that in ancient Greek meant young *lusty* men, they also saved them from catastrophes, did these dolphins and porpoises who of course are not fish, they're warm-blooded and breathe air. Got the picture?"

"No, but I'm impressed," Harold said, truthfully. "Since when did your rakish nature permit scholarship?"

Henry tilted back the *vinjak* bottle before replying.

"In my last residence, in between Cupid's calisthenics, I scoured the extensive classical library."

"Wonderful. But what's this thing got to do with me? And you?"

Henry clapped his bottleless arm around Harold's shoulder and squinted through the dolphin's spray at his brother's owlish face. Yes, he did love this chucklehead.

"Let us go now, you and I," he said. Harold felt himself pulled by Henry's lurch toward a dark side street.

"Dolphins, dolphins, here we come, round the world and we're comin' again," warbled Henry, as he towed Harold. "And the sea shall make ye free," Henry trilled.

Harold pulled away and stood watching his brother wobble farther into the dark street.

"Henry! Henry!"

Henry called back out of the narrow alleyway's gloom.

"C'mon, Harold, c'mon." Harold saw the *vinjak* bottle glinting.

With that destinal feeling filling him, Harold followed. The brothers' steps echoed up from the cobble, and off the stuccoed, balconied Italian façades. Abruptly, Henry stopped and waved his bottle.

"We're here, buddy brother. We're here."

Harold peered at the tall, double wooden door. A bronze dolphin knocker peered back. Henry grabbed its tail and thumped it mightily against the green-gray weathered planking. The booms echoed within and without. Harold cast his eyes toward the black-eye strip of sky that showed between the sheltering pastel buildings. Above the dolphin's echoing song he could hear the sea wash, the counterpoint of voices blown their way, of cars and trucks coughing on the outside of the old town. Vehicles, except delivery vans, were banned here, and as if God had willed it, Harold felt safe in the embrace of something ancient, and the hairs on the back of his neck raised.

"Harold!" his brother cried.

Harold looked, and the sight raised his hairs still further. The greenish-gray doors were swinging inward, creak by creak. Henry pushed forward, arms outstretched like a man who's seen the light. Harold, too, came forward, lured by a cryolacish glow emitting from what looked in the pulsing light like a forest of houseplants and chairs, arranged as if for a wake, except there was no body in the huge foyer, instead a table laden with heaped platters and bottles and glasses, all faintly tinged by the aquaish ether. And into the arms of Henry came, Harold saw, an absolute apparition: A buxom female with red hair turned orange in that odd light, with orange lips and a body sheathed like a knife in an orange dress.

"Harold," mumbled Henry, "meet Thelma Malafort."

The apparition released Henry, turned to Harold and smiled, actually quite sweetly. Harold saw she wore a large gold cross around her neck.

"My pleasure," Thelma said. "Come in, please, and have a bite to eat. Barney's waiting."

"Barney?" Harold blurted, recalling Henry's account of his contretemps with Thelma's religious consort.

"It's OK," Henry said. "New Era stuck. Barney's cool."

"Not between the sheets," Thelma said, taking each brother by an arm.

Inside the large foyer, the light normalized, or perhaps the Venetian chandeliers with their blue-yellow electric tapers just seemed normal now. A large man dressed in black coveralls adorned with an embroidered cross over the left heart pocket advanced from the table, his mouth working on what looked like smoked herring.

"Bounnaaaekl," he seemed to say, swallowing fish.

"This is Barney," Thelma said.

"Barney," the man said, taking Harold's hand and shaking it like a pump handle.

"Harold Fickleman."

"Hi, Barney," Henry said. Harold noticed his brother had sidled slightly behind Thelma.

" 'Lo, Hank," Barney said. "Have a *loza*. I'm not armed. I'm still blissful."

"Glad to hear it," Henry said. "Let's eat, then get to it."

"Oh, Henry," Thelma said, heading for the groaning board, "you're so nice to do all this. To think you'd get rich! To think I went back to Barney!"

"Just thank Dominick's piazza. It really delivered," Henry said. They fell to filling plates and glasses, with Thelma gabbling about her and Barney's flying ministry, and how they'd just loved getting on a plane to come over here and help their dear old friend Henry, but then, couldn't he sell anything to anyone?

"How help?" Harold asked through his Roquefort cheese and black bread.

"God's loose in the world," said Barney. He'd moved on to the Czech ham, Harold saw, and he had Malafort Ministries embroidered on the back of his coveralls.

"Loose, did you say?"

"Loose, Harold," said Barney. "Loose as a goose and twice as crazy."

"Barney's got a way with words," Thelma said. "All evangelicals do."

"Loose! I love it," cried Henry, waving the green *loza* bottle. "Love it, love it, loose! Thelma? For old times?"

"Go ahead, I'm blissful," said Barney.

"How are you going to help?" demanded Harold. "Henry, stay put." Amazingly, his brother and Thelma stopped on their way out of the foyer. "What's going on?" Harold asked. "What is going on?"

Henry and Thelma returned to the table, although Thelma seemed discomfitted.

"All right," Henry said. "Barney, what's the time?"

"Where?" said Barney.

"Oh, for Christ's sake."

"Precisely," Barney said.

"It's 11:30," Thelma said.

"Time then," Henry said. "Barney?"

"Bread on the water," Barney said. Harold watched him lumber out of the foyer and up the side staircase.

"Henry?" said Harold.

"Relax," his brother said. "Thelma. Later, maybe."

"Not a chance," Thelma said. "With you, I'm like Magdalene at the cross."

"Got it!" Barney shouted. He bounded in among them, waving a huge black pistol.

"Oh, God!" Harold said, heading beneath the table. Henry stopped him.

"It's OK, Harold, it's OK, just a flare pistol. Let's go."

Harold again had that funny feeling, all the more intense when the big doors shut behind them and the group began its climb to the wall's top, step at a time, beginning with a dark staircase. Barney led, followed by Thelma, followed by Henry, followed by Harold. Thelma's dress blinked like a beacon in the reflected light from the street lamps.

"Nice ass, eh?" Henry whispered back to Harold. "I swear she can do lazy eights and two-spin rolls with that thing."

"They do look like landing lights," Harold ventured.

At the top of the three-story steps, Barney halted. From the right hip pocket of his Christian overalls he produced a small green bottle. Turning, he waved it at his followers.

"I told you, sir, we are red-hot with drinking," Barney declaimed. "So full of valor that we will smite the air, breathe in their faces, beat the grout, yet always beat toward our project. Onward!"

With that, Barney took a large gulp and, lurching forward, tossed the bottle to Thelma, who gulped and passed to Henry, who largely gulped.

"Wasn't that some bastard Shakespeare?" Harold asked before his gulp.

"Nobody knows Shakespeare's parentage," Henry replied, as they all hurried along the wall toward its southwest corner, facing the bay. Henry prodded Harold with the bottle.

"You'll see," he said. "It's coming down." Harold snatched the bottle.

"Jesus Christ," he said after the stinging potion had cleared his esophagus. "What is that?"

"Special *loza*," Henry said, panting the words because, as Harold scarcely noticed, they were jogging now toward the most southerly point of the wall, overlooking the pleasure boats, yachts, and old coastal defense frigates that the Croats had parked in the inky water. Barney pulled up next to the niche marking the descent into the town. He turned to Henry.

"Oh one-thirty," he said.

Henry nodded, his eyes fixed on the southwest sky. He passed the *loza* to Thelma, who drank and passed it to Barney, who drank and passed it to Harold, who feigned a sip. Then he dropped the bottle in response to Thelma's E-above-high-C screech, "There! There! See?" as she thrust her formidable bosom against the parapet. Harold looked as best he could while Henry was thumping him on the back and shouting, "Yes, by God, yes, there he is!" Barney whooped like a Sioux in a wig factory, and raised his pistol. "Our revels now are started," he cried and squeezed the trigger.

The foursome watched the green flare ascend with its report still echoing in their ears. The light arced like an errant angel returning to home base, trailing sparks that fell toward the now bilious-looking boats, until it reached its apogee, and then it began its slow descent, brighter, slower, so that the entire harbor seemed to flicker like shadows on a cave wall.

"Listen," Henry whispered. They strained forward. Harold heard the bottle shards crunch under his feet and a few far-off exclamations from somewhere in the city. Lovers, perhaps, seeing real fireworks rather than artillery.

"Yes," said Barney. "I hear."

"Me, too," said Thelma. "Oh, Henry, that flare. It was just like a cosmic come, you know?"

"Hush," Henry said. "Yeah, we gotta go. Come on!"

"What?" Harold said, and as he did he heard the engine noise, a low growl, getting louder.

"Ernie, my old flying partner. Come on, we've got to get to the water."

Henry led this time, along the wall to the staircase leading to what once was the south portcullis of the medieval town. Thelma took hold of Henry's belt, and in tow she looked like an orange caboose. But Harold was the real caboose as they clattered down the steps. He was following the Malafort Ministries sign on Barney's back. At the bottom, their heels ringing on the worn cobbles, they sprinted toward the old south exit and, achieving it, came out on the quay facing the pleasure boat basin. Henry skidded to a halt and threw an arm in the direction of Ethiopia. Thelma's momentum took her to the water's edge and, then, with a great orange-bottomed splash, into the bay. Barney whooped and plunged in after her, and in a second emerged with her head firmly grasped by the hair.

"You idiot," Thelma was screaming. "Ape, idiot, let go my hair." But Barney had a death grip and maintained it until he'd grasped the quay's side. Harold watched him sputter and then throw the wailing Thelma up like a sack of grain. He reminded himself not to cross Barney Malafort, even while Thelma was kicking at Barney's hands as her savior pulled himself up.

"Idiot, look what you did, you idiot!" she screamed pulling at the hair out of which the dye was running in yellow rivulets. And then Harold realized that Henry still stood like a statue pointing out over the bay and that the roar of engines was very loud indeed, so loud that it almost, synesthetically, interfered with his sight, whose organs nonetheless were fixed on the majestic sight of a very large seaplane gliding into the water between the rows of boats.

"Goddam! Goddam!" Barney hollered. "Ain't that a for-sure gone-to-Jesus PBY, ain't it?"

"You idiot," Thelma muttered, but she, too, was fixed on the big plane that was cutting the black water into plumed waves as its pilot set it down, feathered the props, and reversed them. The plane rode like a swan toward them like a creature, Harold thought, come to take them to Avalon.

"Come on! Come on!," Henry cried. "The place is swarming with militia and police. Let's go." Henry grabbed Harold's arm and shoved him toward what Harold now saw were steps cut into the sea wall. At the bottom bobbed a dinghy.

"God bless Dominick and Constantina," Henry chortled, as he led them down the wet steps. "Money can buy anything!" Henry helped the dripping Thelma, who looked like a melted orange candle, into the dinghy. Then Harold stepped gingerly into the boat's center. Last to board was Barney.

"Row, Barney, row like you just caught Thelma and me in the last pages of the *Kama-Sutra*!" Henry ordered. And Barney did, bending his back to the chore with an unministerly oath—"One of these days, Fickleman, I'm gonna fuck you with the Word of God!"—and they wobbled off for the plane. Over his shoulder, Harold caught a glimpse of a blue light flashing.

"Cops," Henry said. "Bound to happen. Balkan war nerves."

"Is there a dryer on the plane," Thelma asked. "We have one on *Flying Jesus*."

"Fuck you with the Word of God," Barney heaved, giving the oars a mighty heave that brought them jerking to within ten meters of the PBY's big gray floats.

"Barney," Henry said, "save it for your audiences. Thelma and I is *was*."

That peculiar locution brought them under the plane's sheltering wing, Harold saw, just before he saw the gull-wing cabin door fly up and a most unusual person present himself.

"Henry, you sly, lying son-of-a-bitch, I got her here, didn't I?" said this person, his voice cutting over the thin braccch-braccch of a police claxon. "I got 'em all," the figure shouted from behind goggles that looked like they'd been on the *Spirit of St. Louis*. The rest of the apparition wore a brown, flaking flight helmet—or maybe Red Grange's gameday headgear—and a yellow flight suit with a huge cleaver over the right breast pocket.

"Brother!" called Barney, "Can we come aboard?"

"They have the same tailor," Henry said. "Folks, meet Ernie Butcher, and now let's haul ass."

They did, spurred by blue lights advancing around the point toward the basin.

"Cop launch," Ernie said. "Up and away." Like gymnasts they clambered onto the pontoon, then the foot rests, and on into the fuselage. Harold saw it was bare, as if rigged for cargo.

"Let's do it," Ernie Butcher cried, and he and Henry scrambled for the cockpit. A moment later and the whine of starters had faded into the pop-pop-pop of the Pratt and Whitney twins, and they were turning for the open sea. Harold felt a bit queasy.

"There's no goddam dryer," Thelma said.

"Try this," Barney said, fetching another familiarly green bottle from his overalls. "Make you wet where it counts, dry where it don't."

"Why, thanks, preacher," Thelma said. Then they were all at a thirty-degree angle, bracing against the take-off run, until they felt the big, old seaplane labor into the air, gain some altitude, and level off.

"Arrrrgghhhhhhhh!" cried Barney, grabbing the bottle from Thelma and tipping it back perpendicularly.

"Jesus Christ," Thelma said, "I could troll for fish from here."

Harold struggled to his feet and pulled himself hand-by-hand against the fuselage ribs to a window port. Below, he could see the roiling whitecaps against the black sea and, then just barely visible, a lightening in the east beyond the mountains of Albania. The PBY couldn't have been at more than five hundred feet.

"Not to worry," Henry said, clapping his hand on his brother's shoulder. "Ernie used to dust crops and fly pipeline. We're low so the crazy fucking Albanians don't take us for an attack from their blood enemies, the rest of the world."

Henry, braced against the throbbing wall, turned back for the cockpit. "Why don't you get some rest? We've got to go wide past Corfu so it's about four hundred clicks, an hour, before the next act."

"What act? Henry, damn it, enough! What act? This is all crazy!"

But Henry was already almost to the cockpit. Harold turned toward Barney and Thelma. They lay spooned on the floor, heads against a stack of burlap, Barney keeping the bedraggled Thelma warm. The green bottle rolled against Barney's thigh with each engine throb. Harold felt alone and sad. He crawled to the bottle and took a draught. The fiery *loza* curled down into him and formed a fetus, around which he curled. Then he shut his eyes.

Harold woke to a gentle shake and the words, "Hey, Fickleman, try some of Ernie's fuckin' best Joe." The Styrofoam cup under his nose smelled like coffee baked on the bottom of a Bunn burner. Harold took the cup. "Attaway, Fick," said Ernie. "Set you up for the day." Harold took a swallow. It tasted like ground lava. He saw that Thelma and Barney now were sitting with their backs against the cockpit bulkhead, holding their little white cups.

"Morning," Harold said.

"Just barely," Henry said, poking his head out of the cockpit passageway. "Hey, Ernie, we're there, man. Can you get us down"

"Like rain," Butcher replied, "like fuckin' rain." The pilots re-entered their command center.

"Arrrgghh," breathed Barney, "the Lord's ways are mysterious indeed."

"Damn straight," Thelma agreed. "Where's the *loza*? Hey, Harold, toss the communion wine, will you?"

Harold did, but only after driving the lava out of his throat with a swig. He watched Barney, then Thelma drink, before asking, "What's going on? Do you all know?" The two heads shook in unison, both smiling.

"Ask Henry," the two heads said. Harold looked through the hatch at his brother who was staring through the PBY's canopy downwards. Abruptly, though, as if sensing his brother's scrutiny, Henry swiveled to look directly, deeply into Harold's eyes. Harold nearly flinched, but then the scientist in him, the amoebae man of Uterine Labs, took over. What, he wondered, was behind his brother's eyes? Only the Other?

What Henry saw was his still-jogging-thin brother, Harold, he of the petri dish, of the search for ultimate knowledge. Harold of the sacred intoxication, who once, he'd written Henry, had believed he was priestlike just because he was dressed up like one. He also saw Harold the Lover, who like he, Henry, had mistaken virgins for the Virgin and wives for women. But then, Henry figured, all opposites, all Others, must be linked, or else the binding curve of humanity could not exist. No, whatever God was, It was Otherwise in the extreme. It allowed every kind and shape of human endeavor, each tied in some glorious-hideous arrangement to another, so that a scientist and an RV salesman were both One and Two. Henry smiled at Harold and gave him the thumbs-up signal. The big thing was coming now, the big Other, Henry knew, and then maybe they'd all find out something. Henry felt Ernie's hand on his shoulder.

"There she is, partner, there she fuckin' is," Butcher whispered and took his hand away to point down and left. Andipaxi looked to Henry like an amoeba, although he'd have to defer to Harold on that one. But it was, even at this low altitude, a tiny gray-green blob against the dark sea, a blob just barely lit by the rising sun. A little north glowed a larger blob, the big brother island, Paxi, not that it was much bigger. But it was toward Andipaxi's tiny southeast harbor that Ernie now banked the PBY.

"Yeeehowwwwwww!" came Ernie's cry as they skimmed the

waves. Henry heard Thelma shriek, "Jesus Christ, Barney, that was a flying fish!" and then Barney's basso, "We shall all be fishers of fish if we get any lower," and Harold's gasp, and then exultant, "Henry, we're going down together!"

Henry white-knuckled the co-pilot's wheel watching the island come toward them like a head rising from the sea. He watched Ernie throttle back and bring the nose of the ponderous plane up slightly. The PBY bucked and shuddered hitting the gentle chop, swooshed on, pitching, but Ernie controlled the yaw and the props and, then, throttled way back. The aircraft started to drive like an ungainly barge toward the cove. But toward what? He and Harold had for so many of the past years been driving toward something. Sex? Intoxication? Love and peace? Henry touched Ernie's shoulder.

"Good job," Henry said. "Now we're set?"

Ernie's smile revealed the space where the three teeth he'd lost in Egypt had been. Had it been something about an air pocket? Or was it from tearing off a veil?

"Just like you said, teamwork," Ernie grinned wider, adjusting the variable props to slow the PBY about a hundred yards off the white sand beach. Then he cut the engines.

"Barney!" Henry called. "Get out there and throw that anchor. Harold, get the hatch! Thelma, throw me a bottle, and then push that raft out!"

"Attaway, cap!" Ernie said, pulling off his goggles. "Just like my old partner."

Henry took a long draught before giving the bottle to Ernie. When they'd both drunk, they gave each other the thumbs-up sign before clambering through the fuselage and out into the crisp morning air. Harold, Barney, and Thelma already sat in the big, bobbing, U.S. Navy-issue life raft.

"Hallelujah! We are saved!" Barney cried.

"Not yet," Henry said. "Move over so we can get in this thing."

"I'll paddle," Ernie said. "Old Barn' there may be on speaking terms with Jonah and all that crap, but he rows like a blind fucking farmer."

From his perspective, Harold Fickleman didn't think Ernie was much better. The raft weaved and twirled its way toward shore, but Harold saw they were making progress and the morning was gorgeous. A shimmering light played on the water, raft, trees, sand, and the sun stood high enough so that phenomena were cast in sharp relief; the one blue and white fishing boat riding tethered close to shore; the distant, small onion dome set on the island's middle; his companions, who seemed auraed, a faint blue line around them like TV weathermen against the chromo background. Thelma, he saw, was whispering to Henry and passing him a bottle, while Barney nodded. What now? Harold took a deep breath, and the sharp piney resin came to him and salt air and the faintly rank odor of his body, and the camellia smell of Thelma, counterpointed by Barney's cheesy musk, and Ernie's motor-oil aroma and the sweet-sour waft of Henry that he remembered from their boyhood when in terror of the night or of the terror that came of being orphaned, they huddled against one another beneath the comforter in their grandparents' home. Harold realized the salt smell now came partly from his tears. He wiped them away, pretending something had flown into his eyes.

Then something did fly into his eyes, into all their eyes. The dolphin rose not six feet from the raft, thrusting upward as if launched by a sea god toward the sun, except that the great creature momentarily obscured the sun. The white underbelly threw beadlets of iridescent, ancient water over them. The large mammalian eyes scanned them with inscrutability. The fins flapped as if in greeting before the majestic tail, a yard above the water, guided the dolphin in a downward gliding bank, more graceful than any aircraft. The dolphin's reentry threw a plume of sunlit spray over the raft, which pitched from the impact's ripples.

"Mother of God," Ernie said.

"Sex uncertain," Thelma breathed.

"Something of God," Barney said, his normal PA voice reduced to funereal level.

Henry said nothing but looked at Harold. Again, their eyes locked.

"Protector," Harold said.

"All bets on," Henry now said. "Ernie, row the boat ashore."

They came onto the beach in silence, except for Barney who cried, "I have returned," each thinking, Harold supposed, about the dolphin, about this strange journey, or maybe just about their wet shoes, for Ernie hadn't driven the raft hard enough to beach it entirely. Ten feet onto the sand Henry held up his hand, calling a parley.

"Now, some of you may wonder why I've called this meeting . . . " he began, but then, after a swallow from yet another small *loza* bottle, continued, "OK, follow me."

Harold took up position right behind Henry. Henry, he saw, was tracing footprints, a path, leading from the sand into the pine-tree line, and up into the craggy hills that rose not far from the beach. The group plodded quietly. Ernie, at the rear, kept casting glances back toward the raft and PBY. In the pines they heard gull cries and the small surf and the sound of the needles underfoot and the occasional snatch of birdsong, and, no doubt from the onion dome, windblown fragments of plainsong. Harold saw the sweat break out on Henry's shirt as they labored up the grade into the hills.

"Whew," Thelma said, "only a pig'd want me now."

Barney led the chorus of "oinks," but male laughter died into the pshoosh of the strengthening morning wind moving in the pine tops. Harold felt humbled, as he had on Mt. Athos, as he had in bed with Snezana, as he had, in time almost unremembered, with his lost wife, Mary. Henry arrived at a terrace, or a plateau. The group gathered around him. Harold realized they all were panting, and he could detect the *loza* smell oozing out of them. He also caught a feeling, something like the thrum of a plucked string or the whine of a mosquito. Henry raised his hand then waved his arm in an arc compassing the overgrown rough rock bluff against which the plateau butted, the path up which they'd toiled, the plateau itself, and them.

"Welcome, my friends," Henry intoned, "to the grotto of the dolphin."

With the others, Harold looked around—except for Ernie, who seemed not to be with them, and Harold wondered about that while his eyes traced the cleared space and the vine-draped rock wall, finding nothing.

"Where's Ern . . ." he started but stopped when Thelma cried, "Look! Honey, Barney, look, just like Henry said!" Thelma was hopping on alternate feet, her carmine-nailed fingers pointing down.

"Holy Hot Cross Buns!" Barney responded, and began his own hopping. Henry, meanwhile, bore a pleased look, like a tour guide whose group has, yes, noticed the strange iron tower on the Paris skyline.

"Where's Ernie?" Harold persisted, despite himself studying the ground, where—what was that?—he saw an outline cast by the east-lying sun.

"Where's . . ." but Harold stopped when he saw, and he felt his saliva start. There, faint but clearly discernible in green, blue, red, white mosaic, was the figure of a boy on a dolphin. A boy wearing a coronet, his right arm thrust upward as he rode the breaching dolphin, whose snout was cast backward and up at the boy and whose eyes, of red and white, looked at the rider as if the youth were a sacred treasure. Radiating out from these figures, in lapis lazuli and white, rippled the sea, on whose farthest edge rose the white crescent moon, Harold recognized, of the Great Mother Goddess, originator of the earth, descendent of the Great Egg that rode the brow of the oceans in the beginning, or so the Pelasgians had said—those Pelasgians whose progeny still dwelt, Harold recalled, on

Thassos and Corfu, on many Greek islands, and who believed that they had descended from the mating of the Great Goddess with her first lover, the cosmic snake Ophian. And wasn't that his writhing figure on the opposite edge, in emerald and yellow? But of course that was all mythological drivel, even if all life did originate in the sea, particularly his amoebae, even if there was no doubt about the symbolism of the egg and snake.

"As I said," Henry was babbling, "as I said," and he was laughing and waving now at the rock wall, which suddenly parted before them to reveal Ernie, grinning his spacy grin and waving back at them.

"See, Harold, see," Henry now cried. "This is dolphin island. This is the real place. Here! Right here! The dolphin shrine, sacred to Apollo who once, you know, dwelt in the sea before he became a Sun-God. Apollo, god of healing, music, poetry, health, beauty, . . ."

"And prophecy, praise be!" cried Barney.

"And sex," called out Thelma.

"Love," Harold corrected, realizing suddenly that he, too, was almost hopping around the circle, or at least was shuffling, and certainly sweating.

Henry shouted, "Come on, come on," and with that, Harold's brother plunged toward the waving Ernie by the rock wall. Henry paused to embrace Ernie, and then the two of them turned and disappeared into the wall.

"What?" called Harold, hurrying toward the spot. "Henry? What?" He stopped only to be jostled by the passing Barney and Thelma, Malafort Ministries and orange comet, busting into the wall.

"Harold, hurry now, honey, hurry now," Thelma said. Harold gasped, then caught her elbow, and was pulled into the hanging vine half expecting his nose to flatten against the granite.

Instead he felt the snake-like drag of the vines pushing away and sensed a draught of coolish air and an odor like an attic opened after a long time. And he could see. They were in a fissure, a long crack in the cliff, and above he could see the blue sky through the overgrowing foliage. The passage was wide enough only for a large person, and it was straight. Harold saw the wall was hewn in places, the chisel marks clear and sharp against the gray. Their steps sounded in low thumps against the wall, Barney hurrying and Thelma following and Harold, now detached from Thelma, trailing.

"Oh, listen," Thelma said. "Oh, this is like, well, like . . ."

"Orgasm?" suggested Harold, but he couldn't catch a response because there was noise coming from up ahead, human voices and laughter and the sound of glasses clinking, and was that? Could it be? Children's voices?

"God's Big Bang," Barney called back. "Like God's Big Bang! Snake and egg!"

"Orgasm?" Harold asked again—or had Barney said steak and eggs?—but now the noise made conversation impossible if the half-trotting exertion hadn't. Where had Henry and Ernie gone? What *was* up ahead? He jumped a bit to see over Barney's King Kong head, but needn't have bothered because Barney was coming out into an open area, and now so, too, were Thelma and he, almost careening into it, into the noise, into a circle of rock and a circle of people, only two of whom were Henry and Ernie. And in the center of the circle, my God! reared another boy and dolphin, but this one marble, weathered and ancient. The boy's hand pointed up toward the vault of heaven whirling above the opening. They were inside the cliff, Harold saw. He lowered his eyes to scan the crowd, and then he had trouble seeing through the tears, for there was his one-time wife, Mary, smiling at him, and his children, how big now, how manly and womanly, staring at him as if he had descended from a cloud. And there, just there, was Henry's former wife Helen and their kids, and that must be her Greek, Demetrious. And there, by the statue, sweet Jesus, stood Maynard, holding a Styrofoam wienie like the one Harold had carried to Mt. Athos, the one with the sacred fungus in it. There was Snezana, too, his loving doxie, smiling at him through her full, parted lips, holding a tiny glass up toward him. Surely not the fungus! Oh, no, people could only be God's fools so long, could only bear ultimate truth and joy so long, and then they needed to be just normal for a while. Harold felt his heart pound. What to do? And who were these other Others?

"Harold! Harold! Meet the rest."

Henry's grinning face swam in front of Harold's, the eyes unnaturally bright and wise.

"You remember Helen, and our kids, and that's Demetrious, of course. The svelte creature talking to Ernie is Constantina, a.k.a. Angela Costello, my friend from Naples. That's her bozo husband there chatting up the redhead, who's called Muriel, an old flying pal of mine and Ernie's. Great ass, huh? And the blasted black dude is Melchior. He used to live in a dumpster back home. The lady he's fascinating is called Edna, and she's like Thelma except maybe not as agile. The pouty Eurasian eying the guy with the plastic hotdog—is that Maynard?—is Monique. Getting the picture?"

Harold nodded, even though he didn't quite. He felt the eye-pull of Mary, of the kids, of Snezana, and he saw that everyone was moving into a tight circle around the statue. He saw that each, chatting merrily, held one of the little glasses.

"What?" Harold said. "What . . . but . . ."

"Here, brother, take this." Harold took the glass Henry held out. Henry raised his glass toward the vault of heaven.

"To why we've all come together," Henry said, "and thanks, Ernie, you and the planes, and you, too, Dominick, you great unwilling patron."

The Italian smiled and shrugged, raising his glass yet further.

"To sun, sea, dolphins, Apollo, and this circle," Henry now said. Everyone raised their glasses. Harold could hear the distant sea. He felt rather than heard the inhalations of all the Others.

"But, Henry," Harold cried. "Don't! You don't know. The fungus, it's . . ."

Henry stepped back to Harold, shouldering aside Snezana into the circle next to him. Henry wrapped his free arm around Harold.

"And now, to each's Others," Henry said.

"Zhivili!" hollered Snezana.

"This is your blood!" intoned Barney.

"My body," breathed Thelma.

"Fuckin' A," Ernie said.

"Peace," said Mary and Helen in unison with the children.

"Ya sas," came weakly from Demetrious.

"Cheers," said Maynard, echoed by Monique.

"Amor!" Dominick added.

"Saluda!" said Constantina.

"Mud in your eye," hollered Muriel.

"Lead in your pencil," said Edna.

"God in the sky," bellowed Melchior.

"Henry, what . . ." said Harold.

Henry's face turned full to Harold. He felt Henry's arm tighten around him.

Henry's smile filled Harold's eyes.

"To divine intoxication, Harold. Everybody?"

Harold watched Henry's hand raise his cup, and everyone's hands followed his. He heard Henry say, in a whisper Harold remembered from when they'd hidden under the stairs avoiding retribution for egging the neighbor's car, a whisper saying, "It's OK. Nothing will hurt you. All I, all we, all you, must do is choose."

Then Harold felt his hand bringing the cup toward his mouth. He felt the sun on his shoulders, smelled the sea and pines, heard the birds and faint ethereal chants. He suddenly felt unafraid. Eureka! Euroky! Just choose. He knew his destiny, his last best moment for that had come. Knew it and welcomed it, as he felt the cool edge of the glass scald his lips.

# Memorial Day

Driving into town, he had a familiar, unwelcome sensation: a tingling that always told him he ought to be having some deep emotion, but he wasn't, and so he would, later, be guilty about that. Sort of an early warning system that he hadn't wanted installed. To stop the tingling he turned to the fields stretching away westward beneath the heat shimmers. Corn, mostly, and milo. Some oats. Waving fields that beckoned travelers farther and farther out until the water became scarce, the fields dried to rough pasture, and the mountains rose to mark one part of the world from another. A blast of air-conditioning tickled his nostril hairs, and he was glad he'd never live in this country.

"This is it," he said to her.

"It's like I imagined it," she said. "Has it changed much?" Her short gray-brown hair jiggled now as they hit the cobblestones of the main street.

"I don't know yet," he said. "I haven't been here for fifteen years, and then I was just passing through. Before that, thirty, at my mother's funeral. Forty since my father's."

She smiled. "Why," she said, "that goes back even before you and me."

He watched her eyes scan the block's storefronts: the Big Red Cafe, a ladies' wear store, a Rexall, the Sears outlet, oh, yes, Sears, the REA office, a Farmers Savings branch. Like him, when she held her face down to peer over her glasses, the nascent double chin showed. How strange, he thought, to be irrevocably middle-aged and yet so often feel young, so often feel dumb and vulnerable. He was lucky in one way, she'd said. His hair, graying from its blond, still looked golden in certain lights.

"I'm going to ask at that cafe," he said. He pulled the Chrysler into the curb at an angle.

"Look," she said. "No meters."

"Of course not. Nebraska is God's country. Ask anyone in it. They probably don't even charge interest on loans."

She laughed and looked girlish again. He stepped into the afternoon heat. The air smelled like popcorn, and he remembered that there was a co-op elevator and processor somewhere in town. He ducked under the cafe's awning, pulled, then pushed the door to come into the aromas of coffee and fried foods. The waitress gave him a big grin when he asked directions.

"Which cemetery you want," she said, "Catholic or other?"

"Other," he said. Lord, these native Lutherans didn't even want to be buried next to a Papist. His mother had felt the same, and she'd even been raised Catholic, though with an apostate nature.

"Go down to Sixth Street," the woman was saying. "Turn west and go until you come to Barker's Nursery. Turn north and look west. You'll see the cemetery. Just drive right on in. Can I get you some coffee or anything?"

"No, thank you. I appreciate the information." She smiled again. "I'm visiting my parents' graves," he said, and immediately wondered why on earth he'd told her that. The woman nodded, still smiling. "Thanks again," he said.

He found the Le Baron running. She sat with all the vents turned toward her.

"God, it's hot," she said. "Did you find out?"

"Yes. Do you want to go there now, or should we find a motel and go in the morning? It's pushing five. How about some nice A/C, a few drinks, a swim, and maybe a bit of carnal knowledge?"

Her wide brown eyes inventoried him. A thing he loved in her was the swift, almost always right, instinct.

"Is that what you want? I think you really want to go and look, but you're afraid it'll spoil the day."

"It wouldn't spoil the day," he replied, but he felt himself lying. The trip was a self-imposed duty, he knew, born out of a childhood training that had burned into him the obligation to somehow, someday, honor his father and his mother, and all that was fine, but he'd been supposed to do that while they were alive and he hadn't, and this sentimental journey couldn't redeem that past, but what the hell, he had to do something or his old friend, guilt, would always be with him, dressed in his parents' graveyard clothes, although guilt had a closet full of other garments, and why did he walk hand-in-hand with guilt anyway? Why not just clasp guilt's lesser friend, sorrow, in honor of those people so alive in his memory but so dead just down Sixth Street to the west?

"It wouldn't spoil the day," he repeated. "But I'm whipped. Let's find a place to stay."

There wasn't much to choose from in Glencoe. A Super Eight and a Comfort Inn near the interstate, both crowded with eighteen-wheelers and RVs. Closest to town was a Best Western, huddled like a pre-school Lego building on the west side of the old highway. A south wind chopped the surface of the swimming pool which was hardly bigger than his. That wind chilled, too, after he emerged, chlorined, to stand wondering how many times his father had peered out from his home town at this lowering west sky, the amber-gold going to an amethyst-purple smudge lying like a black snake across the horizon. Hell, the wind stirred his drink. How did people live here?

"What do you suppose my father felt looking at this," he asked her, "day after living day?"

"Didn't he ever say?"

"He never talked about his feelings. I only remember him saying he couldn't wait to leave town."

"And went all the way to Omaha." She pushed her sunglasses up so she could stare at the setting sun.

"Yes. Omaha."

He felt nettled, unreasonably. He held no brief for Glencoe. Or Omaha. He'd spent, or squandered, his life in larger cities around the world. No reason to feel allegiance to this place. Or any other. Not his ground, no more to him, logically, than to the two kids splashing in the shallow end, or to their parents, wide-hipped and road-weary, keeping one eye on their children and the other on their packed car. Minnesota plates, he noticed, and a GO VIKES! bumper sticker.

"When did he leave?" he heard her ask through the gale.

"He went to the University. Then law school. Then Omaha. He wasn't here except for visits, I don't think, after he was eighteen."

She rose from the plastic-latticed lounger to drape a motel towel around her freckled shoulders.

"Well, he's here now to stay. I'm going in. I feel like I'm being blow-dried."

He watched her pick her way barefoot across the hot asphalt, lifting each foot like a show horse. He remembered that: the burnt rubber smell, the sole of your foot or shoe tentacled to it like a piece of pizza lifted from a pan.

Remembered it in New York, Cairo, Singapore, Perth. And so? What good was such a memory? Shouldn't memories be specific, linked to a single place, so that whatever was recalled unsheathed a sword-slash of time past? People who'd stayed put in Glencoe probably had those kinds of memories. He had mental postcards.

He threw back the diluted vodka and tonic. The little Minnesota boy rushed past him to jump in the pool, his mother's eyes checking him over the edge of her Coors Light. The boy, dark against the sunset, froze for a millisecond at the height of his jump. The plummet threw water on the concrete skirt, where it sizzled then evaporated in a skirl of vapor. Boys, water. But in his father's time it was probably a swimming hole on the creek, Beaver Creek the sign said, that threaded the town on its way to the Platte. The Platte River, center line for the Oregon Trail, the proverbial stream too thick to drink, to thin to plow. But OK for wet. He arced the plastic drink cup into the trash barrel.

The room's darkness hurt his eyes. He blinked, found the switch for one over-bed light. She lay curled on her side, dozing. He settled on the edge of the other queen size. How innocent sleeping people always looked, as if just created, no matter what their age. In sleep she looked young again, as when he'd first met her. The lines soft, the tight, anxious look gone. He closed his eyes, trying to force pictures of his children when they were little, asleep with stuffed animals and books and baseball gloves, or cuddling one of the long-dead cats or dogs, and the pictures came, fleeting as eye blinks, in a succession of ages until he saw his daughter and son asleep with their lovers, safe in late-afternoon naps in far-away cites in other countries. He tried to imagine himself as little and asleep, too, with his father watching him, tried to see his father, napping in this town, but he couldn't get either image because he could never see himself or know his father. Maybe to see such things you had to be as innocent as sleepers looked. He stood, moved to the vanity's sinkboard, and mixed another drink. The rattle of the ice disturbed her.

"Hi," she murmured. "I guess the sun got to me." She stretched, bowing her back so that her breasts thrust hard against the bathing suit. Like his mother, she was small boned but well proportioned. He must have been three or four when first he'd noticed his mother's breasts, not in any sexual way, but as a curious feature of her anatomy unrelated to any suckling he might have done. It wasn't until much, much later that he ever tried to imagine his parents making love, so much later it was after his first masturbations, after Joyce whatever-her-name-was had kissed and touched him. Seventh grade? After his father died and his mother remarried, he violently repressed any thoughts of her sexuality. The thought of her writhing beneath the loathsome new husband who'd bought her as surely as any whore brought his gag reflex into full operation, even now. He drained the vodka and tonic.

"Do you want another?" he asked her.

"Please."

He mixed it and carried it to her. Always been good at fetching and carrying. His forte with his mother, during her widowhood, although she made bartending easy, taking her vodka straight except for a dash of bitters.

"Thanks. You look cute in your suit," she said.

"Cute?"

"Sort of grown-up sexy."

"Sort of?"

"Not bad for a middle-aged guy with strong hormones and most of his hair." She put her hand on his genitals. "And only a few extra pounds in the love handles."

"You can't drive a spike with a tack hammer," he said, taking his drinkless hand inside the Lycra to her breast. She shuddered, slapped her drink on the table, and then their four hands were all free and they were out of the suits, on the big bed and into a lovemaking that seemed to take a long time.

They began with her astride him, until he bucked her below him like a good missionary, but they finished in Russian style, she prone, uttering the small cries he always associated with injured animals, and he, his belly bumping buttocks, trying to dam both his orgasm and the unbidden images, for lovemaking should be focused, he professed, and singular, not clotted by the true past of imagined future. But the dam, as always, burst, and he finished while she cried out his name and that of God. Then they lay in the sweat-sheen holding each other in the awkward way of humans returning from the joyous animal to the regretful rational.

"You're wonderful," she said.

"We're wonderful," he corrected without thinking. This duologue they'd often had.

"Whatever."

They lay listening to the air-conditioner throb until it was full dark outside and she disentangled to shower. He made them more drinks. While he bathed, she made more, too. And so they were giddy setting out to find a restaurant. The motel guide proved that a town of seven thousand didn't offer much. He'd settled on a place with the biggest ad, The Last Chance, between Fifth and Sixth streets, a block west of Main. They bumped along the cobbles, made the turn, and came into a large parking lot packed with cars set midway between The Last Chance and the American Legion club.

"One or the other has good food or whores," she said.

"Let's take The Chance," he said.

They found it flossy. Plains Victorian, he could call it. Stained glass, brass fittings, cherry tables, carved wood bar. No Muzak, just the flutings of what must have been 5 percent of Glencoe's population. He put his name on the dining list, and they waited in the bar. He watched her eyes study the people, moving from one to another as though seeking identities. To him they all looked Midwestern Gothic. Women in discount-store dresses or slacks and low-end designer blouses. Men in sport shirts and Sansabelt trousers. Both sexes big and talkative, not afraid to show they ate well or had opinions. A few older men preened in yellow Lions Club tunics festooned with service patches. Yet the crowd looked, he thought, somehow wholesome, as though they'd assembled out of duty.

"Conaway," came the call.

"Age before beauty," he said, sweeping his arm toward the dining room.

"Pearls before swine," she retorted, and they laughed moving into the Last Chance's salon. How sophisticated it was to use the Dotty Parker-Claire Booth Luce repartee. And how irrelevant here. Actually, the Last Chance's extensive menu was pretty sophisticated. He doubted his father had ever had presented in Glencoe choices like braised quail or lemon-pepper sole. No, he bet it'd been sirloin or chicken-fried steak at the Big Red Cafe, over next to Sears.

"So, what will you have?" he asked after their wine arrived.

"Fettucine Alfredo," she said.

"Fettucine? Are you kidding? This is Nebraska, not Italy. You eat meat here. Steaks. Chops. Poultry. Rare beef, cooked pig, breaded chicken. All of them with potatoes and butter and gravy, two vegetables, a salad, and for desert apple pie or crumble with vanilla ice cream. Got it?"

"Fettucine Alfredo."

He waved over their well-fed waitress, and, with a mock scowl, ordered her noodles and a steak for himself.

"What time do you want to go tomorrow?" she asked.

"I don't know. In the morning. I need to buy flowers."

"You'll feel better afterwards, won't you?"

"I hope so," he said, watching her eyes flick to the nearest stained glass. Nerves or avoidance? "Well, different kind of crowd in there, eh?" he said. She took the gambit and they discussed the place and people until the food came.

Miraculously, he thought, her fettucine was perfect. But his steak, ah, that showed Nebraska at its best. The meat had been hung, aged, then broiled just right, so that he could almost feel the animal's strength coming into him. They had brandy with the coffee, and she displayed what she called her Italian Midwesterner balance by taking on the apple pie and ice cream. The bill came to $24.79. In Tokyo, it would have been $247.90.

"Care for a waddle?" He floated the words into the warm, wet evening air to compete with the music billowing from the Legion club. The sad country songs pinged off the parked cars like sonar.

"Sure. I'll work off the pie." They started toward the club.

She hooked her arm around his. "Was Charley Starkweather from around here?" she asked.

"Why, you feeling murderous?"

"No, but was he?"

"Farther west. But he killed some folks on a farm between here and North Platte. He and his girlfriend, what was her name?"

"Carol Fugate. She's out now. Rehabilitated they say."

He sang, "Some people say there's a woman to blame."

"Satan is male," she said.

"Just a big old phallic snake. No wonder Eve couldn't say no."

She moaned, the sound nearly lost in the music as they passed the club entrance.

"Why, why, oh God, isn't there another sex? Where are we going?"

"Just here, out to Main," he said, "then down Eighth."

The street gleamed beneath the lights as empty as if a neutron bomb had radiated all the citizens and left the buildings standing. A few signs glowed. Sears, Rexall, Big Red Cafe, but only the Budweiser sign in the Lincoln Bar and Grill signaled an open business. They walked on, heels clicking, passing the new library, then the Federal style municipal auditorium. He wondered what they might do in there, sheltered from the big sky by the good old WPA workmanship. Built long after his father had left. Besides, his father had hated the New Deal. Took away individualism. But individualism hadn't gotten his father much, or his mother. They'd never owned a house. Didn't have a car all the time he was growing up. They weren't poor, but the American Dream Express never stopped at their door. Had it at his? What would they make of his career? At least he'd made money, not that he was rich, just comfortable enough to indulge himself and a few selected others.

"Stop!" she said. "Smell that!"

Like a whoaed team, they halted on the pitted sidewalk. Lined along the cobbled street stood frame houses, some of them substantial. Sweetgum and cottonwood trees bowered the street. He inhaled. What was it? The scent drove him back in time, tumbling through years, until he could fix it, could feel his skin prickle in emotional time travel. Sure! His grandfather's house, the home of his mother's father. His throat tightened.

"It's columbine," he coughed. "Trumpet vine."

"It's like liquid," she said. "It's all over me like jam. I swear, I feel sweetened."

"Pain in the ass if you let it go because it's hardy. Even grows in this terrible heat."

She tilted her face up to take in the odor. The streetlamp's glare deepened the crow's feet and laugh lines, but her smile smoothed them.

"I forgot," she said, "you know all those gardening things."

He strained toward the nearest house, looking for a number. "OK, just another block."

"What is?"

"The house where my father grew up. 424 East Eighth. It's in the family Bible."

In the evening quiet, their footsteps sounded ominous, but no porch lights clicked on in alarm. Televisions flickered in parlors, as these unafraid folk would call them. An occasional cough drifted from a bedroom, and air conditioners whined against the heat. In one upstairs window he saw a boy hunched over a book, his profile sharp in the gooseneck's light.

"Isn't that it?" she said, pointing to the south side of the street.

It was, the numbers indistinct against the peeling white paint. Three electric meters on the side said the large old place had been divided into apartments, but he saw the wide front porch with its swing still beckoned as if one family lived there. His father probably had leaned against the railing, watching the sky.

"God, it's like an old postcard, isn't it?" she said. He stood staring, hoping to feel something, again trying to force an image he'd never experienced, a memory he'd never had, of his father, of his unknown grandparents, of the equally unknown cousins, aunts, uncles, but nothing came except the here-and-now of an old house in a dying Nebraska town.

"Look," he said. "It's for sale. See the sign?"

"Why don't you buy it?" she said. "Then you'd have something tangible. Isn't that what you want?"

Again, a flash of irritation in him, from her, but she was right to dismiss this like flotsam on someone else's sea. Just an old house. Sure, his father once had ridden a bicycle on that uneven sidewalk, and once the ice and milk wagons clacked down the cobbles to deliver to his grandmother. Once, he knew, there had been a once, at least for them. But for him surveying a dilapidated dwelling on a strange street in a strange town, well, it was like he'd felt on the Sahara. There wasn't any here, here, for him.

"Let's go," he said. They walked without conversation back to the car and in the motel they screwed with almost no sounds, desperately, as if flesh on flesh were an answer, not a question.

He awoke at three, her hot middle pressed against his thigh. What was that low, sireny whistle that awakened him? He strained to place it. Of course. The night wind rushing over the plains, over this low building, running eastward. A signal, he felt. He lifted himself gently from the bed. She stirred, rolled onto her other side. He kissed her shoulder. Then he pulled on his trousers and slipped into a black T-shirt. The Nikes went over bare feet. He closed the door with a soft click and didn't start the Le Baron until he'd coasted away from their room door down the slope toward the motel office. Even this early an ochre knife-edge sat on the eastern horizon. He passed the outlying franchises: a Wal-Mart, a Pizza Hut, a Stop-n-Go, and then the car shuddered on the cobbles of Main Street.

At the intersection of Sixth Street, he started the westward turn. The Sears sign flared at him, suddenly huge and mocking, and he felt his eyes fill with salty water. Forty years ago he'd been there, just a boy, with spending money for the trip from Omaha, with the hearse housing his father, and while his mother negotiated with the monument maker just down the street, he'd bought a primitive electric drill to fix all that had gone wrong. But it hadn't worked, and his mother told him he was heartless to think of such a thing at such a time.

On Sixth, the headlights picked up the lawn ornaments and the eyes of cats left out for the night and the Big Wheels parked on the porches. At the dead end by the nursery, he turned north, then west at the sign. Two hundred yards farther on he came to the cemetery gates, as wide open as the sky. He parked on the road around the curve from the caretaker's office. He took the flashlight from the glove box, and a half-pint of schnapps he always carried. The wind ripped at his clothes as he crunched the river gravel up toward the small outbuilding where they kept the records. He took a pull of schnapps, felt the sweet curl in his throat, a thick coil of heat sidling toward his brain. Mackerel scale clouds scudded across the half-moon.

The warm wind whistled over the old monuments and mausoleums. He stopped for a moment, looking west. They were somewhere in that middle section, he remembered. But where, precisely? Christ, he could remember his Army serial number, and the telephone numbers of people in a dozen countries, and when he'd told his first lie, so why couldn't he recall where the graves were? He moved to the lee of the little office building. Fifty yards beyond he saw the caretaker's bungalow. No light, just the serenity of a home in the early morning hours. He tried the office's door. Locked. Now that was something, he thought, not to trust the dead. He tipped up the half-pint, stashed it in his hip pocket, then slid to the south window. With fingers under the mullions, he heaved upward. The sash moved with a squeak. He shoved the lower sash full open, hearing the weights bang in their channels. He forked his leg through, pulled his torso onto the sill until he felt his right leg touch the floor. Last came his left leg, with the dicey knee from softball played when he was too old for it.

The flashlight showed that the room held only a desk and a typewriter table. But on the desk lay the big records book. So long ago he'd filled out those forms, the data of the dead for the directory of the deceased. He moved the flashlight's beam to the book. The names and locations poured out in alphabetical columns: Anderson, Andrews, Arends, Berry, Buechler, Burnard, Cobb, Cogill, Collicott, Comstock, and then, his, Conaway. He traced his finger along the line. William J. Conaway. His name. His father's name. On the right edge, the plot's location, L-9. He moved his finger to the next line. Conover, But that shouldn't be, he nearly cried out, that shouldn't be, until he remembered that, no, his mother wouldn't be under Conaway. No, she'd had another name when she'd decided she'd had enough of mortality. He fished out the schnapps for a gulp then flipped the pages although he knew she lay next to his father, that he'd insisted on that, that he'd find them together under his name. Maybe he just wanted to feel again the stinging shame of the other name. He found it: Lorainne C. Kohtz, L-9. C for Conaway, not her maiden name. At least she'd held onto the C.

He closed the book and turned to the wall map of plots. There, just down the center roadway to the L-marker, then left a few plots. He slipped the bottle and flashlight back into their pockets before swinging through the window. Carefully, he lowered the sash before scuttling across the driveway and onto the cemetery road. He noticed that the wind had laid a little with dawn approaching, but it still tossed the tree branches and ruffled what was left of his hair. He snapped on the flashlight, slowing his half-trot so that he could see slim white columns by the roadside marking the sections. He was at J. He felt his hard breathing, like a band around his chest. The soft life had done him in. Neither his father nor his mother ever gained an ounce, had walked everywhere, even near his father's end when the cancer ate him through. But with Mr. Kohtz his mother went soft as sin until she'd chosen the fast way of the razor over the slow way of the vodka. Another white shaft reared to his left. The light showed the deep-cut black L. He turned onto the grassy avenue between the headstone rows that in the moonlight looked, in their different shapes and sizes, like some mutant plains crop, or the ranked remains of native idols.

He found the large stone first, between two evergreens. His light played over the chiseled letters spelling their names. Showers of brown needles washed out by the wind fell on and around him. Behind the big marker lay the smaller ones: Lorainne C. Conaway, 1911–1960. William J. Conaway, 1900–1950. The dates seemed deeper cut, as though more important. He now had lived longer than either of them had. An accident of fate. But he had lost their counsel early, never had their approval or disdain for his checkered adulthood. They had never seen their grandchildren. He glanced eastward at the brightening horizon, trying to blink back these tears.

The sun seemed to be rising quickly, as if on a grandfather's clock calendar. Thick black clouds hung in a rope over its slender arc. He looked again at the carved names, and then he drained the schnapps, the liquid flowing into him and over his mouth, down his chin into droplets that fell in silver shards on the green graves' grass. Despite himself the tears fell, too, and he was kneeling between the stones murmuring what he thought might pass for prayers, or apologies. He knelt a long time, until the flashlight's beam was lost in the false dawn.

He stood then and walked to a sprinkler head. He filled the schnapps bottle. Next he went to a plot a few yards away. From the peony bush there he broke off two perfect white blossoms. He thrust their stems into the bottle's neck. At the plots, he put the bottle between the two small markers and stood looking down until a light blinked on in the caretaker's house. Then he walked back to his car. His eyes were clear, and he felt clean, guiltless.

He sat in the motel chair until nine-thirty, when he woke her with their old trick, the rattle of ice in a plastic cup filled with beer.

"Hi," she said. "Want to play?"

"Too late for me," he said. "I've been awake awhile."

"Oh," she said, and rolled out on the other side of the bed.

While she cleaned up, he packed, and after his shower, they drove into town for breakfast at the Big Red Cafe. This time she took the traditional route, ham and eggs and hash browns. He had thick white sausage gravy and biscuits washed down with black coffee. After the waitress cleared their places, she looked directly at him, through him, it seemed.

"Well," she said, "isn't it time for the cemetery?"

He returned the look, seeing that her intuitive sensor, her warning system, was full on.

"No," he said, "what's dead is dead. Let's forget the past."

The sensor processed the words, and her eyes clouded in apprehension.

"Surely," she said, "let's forget it."

They hardly spoke on the long drive back, and when they did it was of little things. The Last Chance, the wind and heat, the cobbled streets. She wore sunglasses all the way, even after dark, all the way into the city and to her apartment. He didn't help her to the door, but she only had her small suitcase. He didn't say he'd call her. He knew that she knew that tomorrow would be a day he needed to be with his wife and children, to check in on life, to let go of all that was at long last dead.

# Moon in Cancer

She told him the news the same way she told him that she loved him: straight, unvarnished, with her brown eyes unclouded. At first he feared he'd gone mad the modern way, because he didn't feel the words, but then he did, and he cried, and held her, and prayed that it would all go away. Of course, it didn't.

They started out going through the well-advertised stages. And through the therapies because they couldn't operate. Too far gone, the surgeons said.

"I don't mind the pain," she told him. "I don't mind losing my hair. I don't even mind having it inside me. What bothers me is that it hates me."

"We'll beat it," he said, almost believing it. "We can beat it." It's what he said every time they talked about the thing that hated her.

The treatments went on, and she felt better. They resumed work, and doing the ordinary things. They went to movies. She started a garden. He played tennis on Saturdays and poker on Thursdays. She went to doctors and to lunch with friends who at first wouldn't talk about her sickness, and then talked about nothing else, hers and others', and how medical science was doing so much now. One day while he was playing tennis he felt a terrible pain in the middle of his chest. It wasn't a heart attack, he knew. It was something else, like panic. And in a moment like smoke dissipating, the pain vanished, and a crazy thought came, like a gift from another time. He stopped in mid-volley, told his friends he'd have to go, and hurried home. She was planting perennials.

"Look," he said. "You're feeling well, right?"

"I feel OK today. Why?"

"We can beat it. We've just got to do something else, that's all."

Then he told her about the pain and the panic, about the recognition he'd had.

"I see," she said. Her brown eyes didn't waver. "So, what else should we do?"

"We'll put something inside you that loves you," he said, "to kill the thing that hates you."

"Oh? Like what?"

"Me, of course." And he grinned until she laughed and hugged him, leaving little muddy marks where her hands had been.

They made love like innocents after that, whenever and wherever they wanted to and could. At lunch they'd frolic in hotels. After work in his office or hers. At home in their bed, on the sofa, and often during the balmy nights outdoors on the soft, moist bluegrass. They relearned the intricacies of the other's body, its locuses of joy, its intersections of discomfort. She learned again his paces, when he felt slow and when he felt as though by sheer force of thrust and love he could overcome the world's way, and she took her pleasure with his. He studied the interstices of her feelings, discovering again how her emotions and her desire were wedded, so that making love was just that, and how if she wept afterward it was as much because her soul had been touched as her body. He watched her grow better, stronger, and happier.

"You know," he said one evening. "We may have discovered the cure."

"What," she smiled. "The Famous Rut Around The Clock Cure?"

"No, I mean it. Look, that guy from the magazine cured himself by watching funny movies, right?"

"Yes."

"And there was that writer who woke up paralyzed and read funny books and got well."

"I remember."

"So, maybe our way is making love . . . me in you, you around me."

"Well," she said again. And again they made love. And again. And again, figuring what the hell, it was something else. A month later, near Halloween, she found that the chemotherapy had not killed all her eggs. Somehow she was pregnant.

"It's a miracle," she said. "A gift. And now I've got yin-and-yang twins in me. One thing's alive, the other's trying to kill me."

No matter. He felt how happy she was. He beseeched her to quit her job. They'd manage, he said, and she needed her strength. Her office gave her a big going-away party and many silly gifts, including a huge, floppy hat to garden in. She bought elastic-waist pants to match the hat, and later, great skirts that billowed around her like sheets blown on a clothesline. They stopped making love except with hands and mouths in the fifth month. Two-thirds of the way through the pregnancy the bad pain started. The doctors gave her pills, but she wouldn't take them.

"I can take it," she told him. "The baby's going to be born straight. No drugs. I can take it."

Now, at night she groaned in her sleep and often awoke. He'd awaken, too, and put his hands on her belly to feel the child toss in its dark, wet world. Sweat came to her temples and browline, and she'd grab the top rail of the old brass headboard and squeeze until he could smell the bad-penny odor of her sweat on the metal.

"Please, please take the pills," he said. "They wouldn't give them to you if they'd hurt the baby."

"No," she'd always say. "I can take it. I'll beat it."

By the eighth month the things in her had worn her down. Around her huge belly her body shrank. Her arms and legs seemed to him like pipe cleaners, and her neck a fragile stalk. She seldom slept now and ate only what she thought the baby needed. Two weeks from term he came home to find her crumpled on the kitchen floor, wriggling like a worm on a fishhook. He didn't listen to her this time, but called an ambulance. In the hospital they put tubes in her arms. She wanted to tear them out, but she was weak, and they told her the baby might die if she didn't let them feed her and give her something for the pain. She lay still, then, every day, waiting, staring at the wall. He took to sleeping in the chair beside her, and he talked to her whenever she'd startle from her trance and say, "Please, say something. It hurts again."

He began telling her stories. The one she liked best she called "the Mexico story." Tell me the Mexico story again, she'd say and manage a small, tight smile.

"OK. Look, after the baby is born and you're stronger, we'll all go to Mexico. We'll fly to the west coast, maybe Acapulco, and rent a car, and go to Zihuantanejo or some little town and we'll rent a villa near the ocean. It'll be mid-summer, see, during your sign, so the living will be easy. The baby will sleep in a little woven basket, and we'll sleep in a huge wooden bed with a mosquito curtain like in *Night of the Iguana*. We'll eat lots of fresh fruit and seafood and get lots of sun. We'll go out deep-sea fishing, and we'll swim in the warm sea every day and play with porpoises. Our hair will bleach out white. We'll drive to the ruins, too, to inland places like Oaxaca. We'll drive all around with the baby, and we'll have the world's best suntans. We'll take lots of vitamins, and we'll make love every day, just like we did before, and when the moon's full we'll go outside into the tropical flowers, into the cool, and do it in the silver light. You'll get better and better, and finally you'll be all well."

She'd smile then, or even laugh.

"You're a great storyteller, you know," she'd say. "The baby'll like that. But you left out the doctors. Tell about the doctors."

"Oh, yeah, I forgot them." He hadn't, of course, but it was a game they played, and it made the story longer and the waiting less hard.

"We'll find all the good love doctors down there. Not the ones with the hormones and the apricot pits and the implantations. The ones who know about love-life. And then, every three months or so we'll come back to the U.S. for a visit, and to show the baby his native country . . ."

"Or *hers*."

"Right, or hers. And we'll take you around to all the clinics and hospitals and doctors and show you off, how healthy you are, how brown like a rich lady, and how the baby can speak two languages, and we'll tell them about our cure, about the love cure. See? It'll all work out fine. Hey! The good Mexican doctors know this stuff. They're Latin. Very romantic."

She laughed then and said something like how those doctors should have treated Steve McQueen. He told the Mexican story two or three times a day, sometimes adding places, or changing the destinations and details, but basically he told it the same way because she liked it not to change much.

Three weeks after she'd come to the hospital, her labor pains started.

"I'm so glad," she said, between them. "It's a better pain. It's worth something." She labored all one day, and part of the night. But she was so weak that she couldn't deliver, the doctors thought. They wanted to take the baby out of her.

"No, please. No, just let me keep trying." She cried then, and he wouldn't let them cut her open. He just held her hand, and prayed, and looked out the window at the deserted moonlit street. She kept pushing, and now her hair shone wet with sweat, and her wiry arms shook with each pain, and her legs trembled and cramped. The nurse shook her head, her eyes saying they were both crazy. The pains finally got very close together, and, relieved, they all went to the delivery room. He stood close to her head, and held her hand. She panted, gasped, cried out horrible frightening shrieks, but the baby wouldn't come. Just push, push as hard as you can, the doctor said, just push, for God's sake, it's coming, just push, please, just push.

He stood, trembling himself, and crying because it hurt her so much, and then he felt something strange. Her hand, the one without the tubes, was at his fly. She was trying to unzip it.

"Please," she whispered to him. "Please." The sweat beaded on her upper lip, and then her face contorted with another contraction. He unzipped, and put her hand inside. He felt her fingers close around his penis, and despite himself, he felt aroused, there in the cold room, with the doctor and the nurses looking at them in surprise and disgust, there in the birth and medicine odors and in the bright light over her tented knees. He became warm and erect, her hand contracting around him.

"It works," she said. "Staff of life," she said.

She pushed then, as hard as she could, gave a cry, and their baby cascaded into the light, bloody and wrinkled but whole and alive, propelled into the world of pain and hate, of joy and love. A solstice child, for sure, he thought.

"I'll be damned." the doctor said. "A girl. It's a girl. I'll be damned."

She released the pressure of her hand then, groaned a little laugh, and with the smallest shudder turned away to defy the hateful thing still inside her.